THE DETECTION COLLECTION

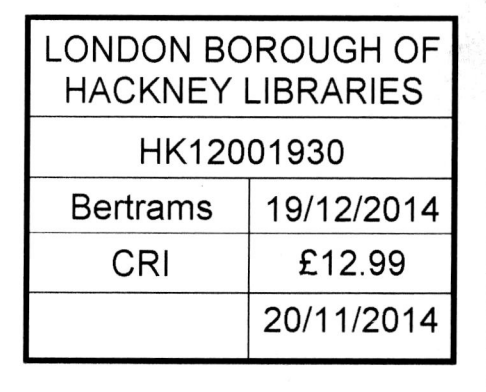

EDITED BY SIMON BRETT

THE DETECTION COLLECTION

ROBERT BARNARD

LINDSEY DAVIS

COLIN DEXTER

CLARE FRANCIS

ROBERT GODDARD

JOHN HARVEY

REGINALD HILL

P.D. JAMES

H.R.F. KEATING

MICHAEL RIDPATH

MARGARET YORKE

HarperCollins*Publishers*

HarperCollins*Publishers*
77-85 Fulham Palace Road
Hammersmith, London W6 8JB
www.harpercollins.co.uk

This edition published 2014
1

First published in Great Britain by
Orion 2005

ISBN 978-0-00-758389-8

Printed and bound in Great Britain by
Clays Ltd, St Ives plc

To all the members, past and present,
who have contributed to the unique history of
the Detection Club

CONTENTS

INTRODUCTION

Simon Brett

This volume of crime stories was originally published in 2005, arguably to celebrate the seventy-fifth anniversary of the founding of the Detection Club. At that time I used the word 'arguably', not because the occasion did not qualify for celebration, but because there is argument about the precise date of the Club's inauguration. (For further details of this, consult *The Detection Club – A Brief History* at the back of the book.)

So this new edition could be said arguably to celebrate the Club's eighty-fifth anniversary. But in all those many years of existence, the primary distinction of the Detection Club has not changed. When founded in 1930 – or 1929 or 1932, according to different authorities – its membership comprised the cream of British crime-writing talent, and that is still the situation today. As a result, *The Detection Collection* has an extremely distinguished list of contributors.

In my role as editor – and, incidentally, the Club's president – I had the great pleasure of being the first to read the stories as they were delivered. And I remember being delighted, not just by the quality, but by the variety of the contributions. Each one reflected the unique voice of its author.

There were stories of devilish cunning, as one would

expect from the minds of P.D. James and Colin Dexter. There were lighter-hearted contributions from H.R.F. Keating, Lindsey Davis and Robert Goddard. Michael Ridpath presented a story of skulduggery in the corporate world he knew so well. Robert Barnard's skills as a literary historian were focused on a slightly fictionalised incident in the life of Henrik Ibsen. Clare Francis provided a chilling character study.

And some of the contributing authors wrote new stories about well-loved serial characters. Margaret Yorke went back to the beginning of her distinguished crime-writing life with a story featuring her academic investigator Patrick Grant. John Harvey revived the career of jazz-loving Charlie Resnick, and Reginald Hill provided the delicious rarity of a story featuring Dalziel without Pasco.

Sadly the passage of the years means that some of the contributors are no longer with us. H.R.F. Keating, Margaret Yorke, Reginald Hill and Robert Barnard will not be delighting us with any new investigations, but they do live on through the quality of their work

And they all added to the wonderful mix of *The Detection Collection*, which still represents the very best in contemporary crime fiction. I am confident that you will get as much pleasure from the stories as I did when I first read them.

THE PART-TIME JOB

P.D. James

By the time you read this I shall be dead. Dead for how long, of course, I cannot predict. I shall place this document in the strong room of my bank with instructions that it shall be sent to the daily newspaper with the largest circulation on the first working day after my funeral. My only regret is that I shan't be alive to savour my retrospective triumph. But that is of small account. I savour it every day of my life. I shall have done the one thing I resolved to do when I was twelve years old – and the world will know it. And the world will be interested, make no mistake about that!

I can tell you the precise date when I made up my mind that I would kill Keith Manston-Green. We were both pupils at St Chad's School on the Surrey borders, he the only child of a wealthy businessman with a chain of garages, I from a more humble background, who would never have arrived at St Chad's except for the help of a scholarship endowed by a former pupil and named after him. My six years from eleven to seventeen were years of hell. Keith Manston-Green was the school bully and I was his natural, almost inevitable victim: a scholarship boy, timid, undersized, bespectacled, who never spoke of his parents, was never visited at half-term, wore a uniform that was obviously second hand and was, like the runt of the litter, destined to be trampled on.

For six years during term-time I woke every morning in fear. The masters – some of them at least – must have known what was happening, but it seemed to me they were part of the conspiracy. And Manston-Green was clever. There were never any obvious bruises, the torment was subtler than that.

He was clever in other ways too. Sometimes he would admit me temporarily into his circle of sycophants, give me sweets, share his tuck, stick up for me against the other boys, giving hope to me that all this signalled a change. But there never was a change. There's no point in my reciting the details of his ingenuities. It is enough to say that at six o'clock in the evening on the fifteenth of February 1932, when I was twelve years old, I made a solemn vow: one day I would kill Keith Manston-Green. That vow kept me going for the next five years of torment and remained with me, as strong as when it was first made, through all the years that followed. It may seem odd to you, reading this after my death, that killing Manston-Green should be a lifelong obsession. Surely even childhood cruelty is forgotten at last, or at least put out of mind. But not that cruelty; not my mind. In destroying my childhood, Manston-Green had made me what I am. I knew, too, that if I forgot that childish oath I would die bitter with regret and self-humiliation. I was in no hurry, but it was something I had to do.

My father had inherited the family business on the fringes of London's East End. He was a locksmith and taught me the trade. The shop was bombed in the war killing both my parents, but government money compensated for the loss. The house and the shop were rebuilt and I started again. The shop wasn't the only thing I inherited from that secretive, obsessive and unhappy man. Like my father, I too had a part-time job.

Through all the years I kept track of Keith Manston-Green.

I could, of course, have received regular news of him by placing my name on the distribution list for the annual magazine of St Chad's Old Boys Society, but that seemed to me unwise. I wanted St Chad's to forget I had ever existed. I would rely on my own researches. It wasn't difficult. Manston-Green, like me, had inherited the family business and, motoring through Surrey, I would note every garage I passed which bore his name. I had no difficulty, either, in finding out where he lived. Waiting for my Morris Minor to be filled, I would occasionally say, 'There seems to be quite a number of Manston-Green garages in this part of the world. Is it a private company or something?'

Sometimes the answer would be 'Search me, Guv, haven't a clue.' But other times I got a nugget of information to add to my store.

'Yeah, it's still owned by the family. Keith Manston-Green. Lives outside Stonebridge.' After that it was only a question of consulting the local telephone directory and finding the house.

It was the kind of house I would have expected. A new red-brick monstrosity with gables and mock Tudor beams, a large garage attached which could take up to four cars, a wide drive and a high privet hedge for privacy, all enclosed in a red-brick wall. A board on the wall said in mock antique script, *Manston Lodge*.

I wasn't in any particular hurry to kill him. What was important was to make sure that the deed was done without suspicion settling on me and, if possible, that the first attempt was successful. It was one of my constant pleasures, scheming over possible methods. But I knew that this mental anticipation could be dangerously self-indulgent. There would come a moment when planning, however satisfying, must give way to action.

When the war broke out in 1939 my fear, greater than

that of the bombing, was that Manston-Green would be killed. The thought that he would die in action and be remembered as a hero was intolerable, but I need not have worried. He joined the RAF, but not as a flier. Those coveted wings were never stitched above the breast pocket of his uniform. He was a Wingless Wonder, as I believed the RAF called them. I think he had something to do with equipment or maintenance and he must have been effective. He ended as a wing commander, and naturally he kept the rank in civilian life. His sycophants called him the Wingco – and how he revelled in it.

It was in 1953 that I decided to begin taking active steps towards his elimination. The shop was modestly successful and I had a manager and an assistant, both reliable. My part-time job was an excuse for short absences and I could confidently leave them in charge. I began making short visits to Stonebridge, a prosperous town on the fringes of the commuter belt where my enemy lived. Perhaps the words 'held court' would be more appropriate. He was a member of the local council and of one or two charitable trusts, the kind that confer prestige rather than making unwelcome financial demands, and he was captain of the golf club. Oh yes indeed, he was the 'Wingco', strutting about the clubhouse as he must once have strutted in the Mess.

By then I had discovered quite a lot about Keith Manston-Green. He had divorced his wife, who had left him taking their two children, and was now married to Shirley May, twelve years his junior. But it was his captaincy of the Stonebridge Golf Club that gave me an idea how I could get close to him.

I could tell within five minutes of entering the clubhouse that the place reeked of petty suburban snobbery. They didn't actually say that no Jews or blacks were permitted but I could tell that there was a set of clearly understood conventions designed to enable the members to feel superior to all but the chosen few, most of them successful local businessmen. However, they were as keen on increasing their income as were less snobbish enterprises and it was possible to pay green fees and enjoy a round, either alone or with a partner if one could find one, and to take lessons from the pro. I gave a false name, of course, and paid always in cash. I was exactly the kind of interloper that no one took much notice of. Certainly no one evinced any desire to partner me. I would have my lesson, drink a solitary beer and quietly depart. The undersized, ordinary-looking, bespectacled boy had grown into an undersized, ordinary-looking, bespectacled man. I had grown a moustache but there was otherwise little change. I had no fear that Manston-Green would recognise me but, taking no risks, I kept well out of his way.

And did I recognise Manston-Green when I first saw him after so many years? How could I fail to do so? He too was a grown-up version of the tormentor of my childhood. He was still tall but stout, carrying his stomach high, red-faced, loud-voiced, the black hair sleeked back. I could see that he was deferred to. He was the Wingco, Keith Manston-Green, prosperous businessman, provider of jobs and silver cups, slapper of backs, dispenser of free drinks.

And then I saw Shirley May, his second wife, drinking with her cronies at the bar. Shirley May. She was always called by that double first name, and behind her husband's back I occasionally caught their salacious whispers, 'Shirley May, but on the other hand, she may not!' He had got his trophy wife, blonde, though obviously not naturally so, voluptuous, long-legged, a second-hand film-star vision of feminine desirability. Even to look at her, standing at the club bar flirting with a group of bemused fools, made me sick. It was then that I first began to see how I might kill her husband. And not only kill him, but make him suffer over months of protracted agony, just as he had made me suffer for years. The revenge wouldn't be perfect, but it would be as close as I could get.

The months I spent leading up to action had to be carefully planned. Firstly, it was important that Manston-Green did not see me, or at least not close enough to recognise me, and that he never heard even my false name. That wasn't difficult. He played only at weekends and in the evenings; I chose Wednesday mornings. Even when our visits had coincided, the Wingco was far too important to cast his eyes on undistinguished temporary players only permitted on the greens because their fees were needed. It was important, too, that I didn't become even remotely interesting to other members. It was necessary to play badly, and on the few occasions that someone condescended to partner me, I played badly. That took some skill: I naturally have a very good eye. I had my story ready. I had an elderly and ailing mother living in the neighbourhood and was paying occasional dutiful visits. I embarked on boring descriptions of her symptoms and prognosis and would watch their eyes glazing over as they edged away. I kept my appearances infrequent; I did not want to become an object of gossip and curiosity even if both were dismissive. I needed to be too anonymous even to be regarded as the club bore.

Firstly, I needed a key to the clubhouse. For a locksmith that wasn't difficult. By careful watching I discovered that three people had keys, Manston-Green, the club secretary Bill Caraway, and the pro, Alistair McFee. McFee's was the easiest to get my hands on. He kept it in the pocket of his jacket which he invariably hung on the door of his office. I bided my time until, one Wednesday morning when he was occupied on the first green with a particularly demanding pupil, with gloved hands I took the key from his pocket and, locking myself in the lavatory, took an impression. On my next visit, surreptitiously, I tested the key. It worked.

I then began the second part of my campaign. Late at night, alone in my London office and wearing gloves, I cut out words from the national newspapers and pasted them on to a sheet of writing paper, the kind sold in every stationer's shop. The message, which I sent twice weekly, had small variations of wording but always the same insinuating poison. *Why did you marry that bitch? Don't you know she's having it off with someone else? Are you blind or something? Don't you know what Shirley May's up to? I don't like to see a decent man cheated. You should keep an eye on your wife.*

Oh, they had their effect. On subsequent visits to the golf club when, carefully distanced, I watched them together, I knew that my carefully calculated strategy was working. There were public quarrels. Members of the club began to edge away when they were together. The Wingco was rattled – and so, of course, was she. I gave that marriage no more than two months. Which meant that I couldn't delay.

I fixed the actual date two weeks ahead. Only one other thing was necessary. I made sure that the new clubs I purchased were the same make as his, a necessary extravagance. I substituted my driver for his driver, handling it always with gloves. It was his prints I wanted, not mine. I made sure my final messages were received on the morning of the crucial day, his by post, hers pushed under the door when, watching, I saw him drive away for work. Hers said, *If you want to know who's sending these notes, meet me in the clubhouse at nine tonight. Burn this note. A friend.* His said the same, but gave a time ten minutes later.

I realised, of course, that neither might come. That was a risk I took. But if they didn't, I would be in no danger.

It would simply mean that I needed to find another way of killing Manston-Green. I hoped it wouldn't be necessary. My plan was so perfect, the horror I had planned for him so wonderfully satisfying.

I won't distress you with details; they are not necessary. I had my keys to the clubhouse and I was waiting for her, her husband's driver in hand. As I said, I have a good eye. It took only two swings to kill her, three more to batter her face into a pulp. I dropped the driver, let myself out and locked the door. There was a public phone box at the end of the lane. When I asked for the police I was put through promptly and without trouble. I disguised my voice although it wasn't strictly necessary. It became the confused, high-pitched, terrified voice of an older man.

'I've just passed the golf club. There's screaming in the clubhouse. A woman. I think someone's killing her.'

'And your name and address, sir?'

'No, no. I'm not getting mixed up in this. It's nothing to do with me. I just thought I ought to let you know.' And with gloved hands I rang off.

They came, of course. They came just in time to see Manston-Green bending over his wife's body. I couldn't have planned that. I imagined they might have been late but would still have had the club with her blood and matted hair, the fingerprints, the evidence of quarrels. But they weren't late; they were just in time.

I resisted the temptation to go to the trial. It was irritating to have to forego that pleasure, but I thought it prudent. Press photographs were being taken of the crowd, and although the chance of being recognised was infinitesimally small, why risk it? And I thought it sensible to continue going occasionally to the golf club, but less frequently. The talk was all of the murder, but no one bothered to include me. I took my solitary lessons and departed. He appealed, of course, and that was an anxious day for me. But the appeal failed and I knew that the end was now certain.

There were only three weeks between sentence and execution and they were probably the happiest of my life, not in the sense of an exultant joy, but of knowing myself at peace for the first time since I'd started at St Chad's. The week before the execution I was with him in spirit through every minute of every hour in that condemned cell. I knew what would happen on the morning when he would be launched out of this world and out of my mind. I pictured the arrival of the executioner the day before to fulfil Home Office requirements: the dropping of a sandbag in the presence of the governor to make sure that there would be no mishap and that the length of the drop was correct. I was with him as he peered through the spy-hole in the door of the condemned cell, a cell only feet away from the execution chamber. It's a merciful death if not mishandled and I knew Manston-Green would die with less pain than probably would I. The suffering was in the preceding weeks and no one could truly experience that horror but he. In imagination I lived his last night, the restless turning and twisting, the strengthening light of the dreaded day, the breakfast he wouldn't be able to eat, the clumsy kindness of the constantly watching guards. I was with the hangman in imagination when he pinned Manston-Green's arms. I was part of that little procession which passed through the dreaded door, the white-faced governor of the prison present, the chaplain keeping his eyes on his prayer book held in shaking hands.

It's a quick death, only some twenty seconds from the moment the arms are pinioned to the drop itself. But there would be one moment when he would be able to see the scaffold, the noose hanging precisely at the level of his chest before the white hood was pulled into place. I exulted at the thought of those few seconds.

As usual I went to the prison the day before the execution. There were things to be done, instructions to be followed. I was greeted politely but I wasn't welcome. I knew they felt contaminated when they shook my hand. And every prisoner in every cell knew that I was there. Already there was the expected din, shouting voices, utensils banged against the cell doors. A little crowd of protesters or morbid voyeurs was already collecting outside the prison gate. I am a meticulous craftsman, as was my father before me. I am highly experienced in my part-time job. And I think he knew me. Oh yes, he knew me. I saw the recognition in his eyes that second before I slipped the white hood over his head and pulled the lever. He dropped like a stone and the rope tautened and quivered. My life's task was at last accomplished and from now on I would be at peace. I had killed Keith Manston-Green.

PARTNERSHIP TRACK

Michael Ridpath

'I've had a dozen interviews here and in New York, I've met the head honcho twice and he loves me, everyone else thinks I'm perfect for the job, so tell me why I shouldn't take it.'

We were sitting in 'The Bunker', the wine bar beneath the twenty-six-storey office block in Bishopsgate that Peter Brearton and I had occupied along with a few hundred other bankers several years before. Between us were two glasses, empty, and two bottles of Sancerre, one empty and one half-full. I refilled Peter's glass. Peter was ambitious, energetic, highly intelligent, unfailingly successful in everything he did. He was thirty-one, a year older than me, although he looked younger, with his square face, short blond hair and round glasses. He was mellowing as he often did after a bottle of wine. I would get to the truth.

'Don't you trust me?' he said.

'Of course I trust you. I trust you more than anyone else I know. We're old mates. That's why I want you to explain to me why you left.'

Peter shook his head. 'I told you, I can't tell you.'

'They've got a great reputation,' I went on. 'They're aggressive but fair, they're cunning but people trust them. They might not be big, but they're the best in the world in their market. Bill Labouchere is a genius. Everyone says so.'

'Don't do it,' Peter said.

I took a deep breath. 'My boss gave me a month to find another job.'

Peter raised his eyebrows. I squirmed. It was something I hadn't wanted to admit. A last resort.

'How long ago was that?'

'Three weeks.'

'Oh.' He took a sip of wine. 'Still don't do it.'

I couldn't conceal my frustration. Labouchere Associates was a small elite outfit that had been responsible for some of the most daring takeovers and mergers in the oil business of the last decade. And they paid well. I would be doubling my salary as a vice-president. Partners, of whom there were a dozen or so, were reputed to earn many millions of dollars every year. That was certainly something to aim for. And the only thing that was standing between all that and me was Peter's opinion.

'I'm going to take it,' I said.

Peter shook his head sadly. 'You're making a big mistake.'

'If you can't give me a good reason not to, I'm taking the job.'

Peter drained his glass, and stared at me thoughtfully. 'All right,' he said. 'I'll tell you. But first get us another bottle of wine.'

He began:

It was last February. I had been at Labouchere just over two years and I was doing pretty well. The firm usually promotes new partners in March, and that year there was only one opening. They take the process very seriously, too seriously according to some of the partners, but not according to the only one that matters, Bill Labouchere. He insists on a weekend off-site session of role play, where the vice-presidents on the partnership track are put through a string of exercises, all watched closely by him and one other partner. The sessions are notorious within the firm, but unavoidable if you want promotion. And believe me, we all wanted promotion.

There were six candidates. Labouchere prides itself on its international staff: there were two Americans, a Canadian, a Colombian, a Norwegian and myself. The session was to be held at Lake Lenatonka, some godforsaken camp in New Hampshire. I flew over from London to Boston and drove a hired car from there all the way up to the lake. I was knackered, I had been pulling several all-nighters on a big financing project we were setting up in Rajasthan. Believe me, the last thing I was in the mood for was corporate games.

Lake Lenatonka was fifteen miles off the main road, down a dirt track in what they call the White Mountains. And they *were* white, or at least a blue shade of white in the moonlight. I didn't pass a single car on that track, just pine trees, thousands and thousands of pine trees. I stopped every couple of miles to check the map. I dreaded getting lost; I could easily spend the whole night driving around those back roads without seeing anyone.

It takes a long time to drive fifteen miles along a dirt track at night, and I was relieved when I saw the wide expanse of the lake, a white board of snow on ice. The camp was a series of a dozen log cabins clustered around a larger building, from which a welcoming column of smoke twisted. There was indeed a roaring log fire in the reception and I went straight in to dinner, which had started without me.

The five other candidates were there, with Steve Goldberg, one of the partners, and Bill Labouchere. Everyone, even I, was wearing American corporate casual clothes: chinos and designer button-down shirts. It was warm, the drink was flowing and we were all having a great time. You've met Bill; he can be charming when he wants to be and he knows how to relax people. He's a Cajun, from Louisiana, you know, that's where he gets that weird accent. His father has his own oil company and sent him to Yale and then Columbia, where he read Psychology. He only went into the oil business himself when his father's company ran into trouble. He couldn't save it, but he did learn how to do deals. He's the expert at doing the deal. The thing to remember about Bill is that it's impossible for you to read him, but he can read you like a book.

It was a great dinner, exquisite food, wonderful Californian wines, Armagnac, cigars, we were all having a good time. I was sitting next to Manola Guzman. She's a Colombian from the New York office, very smart, very poised, with dark flashing eyes, as sexy as hell. She speaks perfect American English with only the trace of a Latin accent. Her father is high up in the Colombian national oil company and she joined Labouchere out of Harvard Business School. She had a very good reputation, although people said that when she lost her temper she became quite scary. We hadn't worked together much before, but she and I got on well that evening. I was enjoying myself. So was Bill, on her other side; the two of them were charming the pants off each other. He's maybe sixty-two, but he's quite handsome with his tanned face, black eyebrows and that shock of thick white hair. He had just ditched wife number three.

Then Bill made his speech. It was only a short one; he basically said two things. Firstly, we would all receive a package of information to study overnight, a 'case'. We would be divided into three teams of two and would role-play a takeover battle. This was bad news: I was shattered and now a little drunk, not at all in the mood for reading documents late into the night.

Then came the second announcement. 'You've all come a long way for this weekend,' he said. 'I would like to thank you for that. I know you are working on some very import-ant transactions.' We all tried to look important. 'But I think it only fair to let you know who it is you have to beat. You all have a chance to make partnership, that's why you are here, but one of you is in pole position.'

Suddenly we were all sober. Bill let the moment rest. He had that frustrating, slightly amused look on his face that he wears when he's playing with you. We glanced around the table. There had been much office gossip about who would be promoted, and frankly I considered myself the favourite, with Manola and a Canadian smooth-talker called Charlie Cameron close behind.

'Harald Utnes,' Bill said. There was an intake of breath around the table. Eyebrows were raised. I noticed Manola next to me give a little smile. Perhaps she was pleased that my name hadn't been mentioned. I knew Harald well. We had worked together for a year in London before he moved to New York nine months before. He was a tall Norwegian, a very nice guy, a geologist, totally reliable, but in my opinion he lacked the killer instinct, the ability to close a deal. And in our business, it's closing deals that makes the money.

Deflated, we staggered outside and over to our cabins, clutching the sheaf of overnight reading. Scattered lights illuminated the path, but beyond them was the night, the stars, the snow, the millions of trees, the great American wilderness. Four of us peeled off in the same direction, Manola, Harald, Trent Dunston, an Ivy League jock from the New York office, with blue eyes, a turned-up nose, gleaming teeth and a scheming brain, and myself bringing up the rear. We were all a little drunk, but Trent was drunker than the rest of us.

'Good night, Manola,' he said. 'Good night, Harald. Sleep well, both of you.' His words were laced with innuendo.

Manola stopped in her tracks. 'Fuck off, Trent,' she snapped, anger igniting in her voice. 'If you can't accept reality, that's your problem, not ours.'

Trent looked meaningfully at me and disappeared off to his cabin. Manola noticed my presence and looked confused. 'Sorry,' she said. 'Good night, Harald, Peter.' And we all retired to our separate cabins. My interest piqued, I dawdled on the way to mine, just to make sure.

My alarm went off at four, and I got stuck into the case. Two oil companies, one French and one American, were competing to buy drilling rights in the Peruvian rain forest. Harald and I were to play the role of the French company. It was fiendishly complicated. To the usual problems of reliability of reserves, valuation and negotiation strategy, were added an ethical minefield of officials to bribe, public-relations pitfalls and environmental risks.

I was exhausted. My head throbbed and my eyes hurt, but at least I had the five-hour time difference on my side. At a quarter to six I noticed a tinge of grey around the edges of my curtains and decided to go for a half-hour run to clear my head.

I set off down to the lake and ran for about a mile along the shore on a path beaten into the snow. The dawn crept pink over the mountains to the east, and I fell into a rhythm, my breath puffing in clouds in front of me like an ancient steam train. All was quiet around the lake, all was peaceful. The first half mile was bitterly cold, but once I warmed up the sharp air was invigorating. As I ran, it suddenly occurred to me that the case was a trap. The smart thing to do was not to bid for the Peruvian oilfield at all: it would cause more public relations headaches than it was worth. I grinned to myself, it was typical of the kind of test Bill Labouchere would set. Well, I would show him that I could step back and see the bigger picture.

On my return journey I met Trent powering towards me: he had turned left along the lake shore where I had turned right. He slowed up so that we would meet, wished me a good morning and then pulled away. There was no doubt that he was fitter and stronger than me. And, competitive fool that I am, it pissed me off.

As we ran past the main lodge I saw a grey four-wheel drive speeding down the dirt track towards us. I wondered vaguely who it was arriving so quickly at that time in the morning, but I was too wrapped up in the case to give it much thought. I had a shower in my cabin, and walked back to the lodge for breakfast, my brain buzzing with PR strategies to ambush my American competitors when they bid for the Peruvian oilfield.

I knew something was wrong as soon as I walked into the dining room. The shock was palpable. The mountainous paraphernalia of an American breakfast buffet was untouched.

'What is it?' I asked Manola, who was standing, stunned, at the edge of the group, next to a large ham.

'Harald has been killed.'

'What!'

'He was found by the lake, early this morning. He was murdered.'

'No! Oh, my God.' I looked at Manola. Her bottom lip was shaking: she bit it to keep it still. I touched her arm. 'I'm sorry.'

She took a deep breath and fought to compose herself. She succeeded. 'Peter?' she said quietly, looking ahead of her, blinking.

'Yes?'

'You may have guessed something about me and Harald, I don't know, you may not have. But if you have, don't tell anyone, please. I'll do it, once I've figured out how.'

I looked at her sharply. From Trent's comments the night before and Manola's response, I had guessed there was something going on between Harald and her. People abandoned their social life at companies like Labouchere, men and women spent long days, and nights, working together on deals; it was easier to begin a relationship inside the firm than outside it. That kind of thing was heavily frowned upon at Labouchere Associates. I had no doubt that if Bill found out about it, both of them would lose any chance of partnership. But someone had been killed, for God's sake! Would Manola still try to salvage her partnership hopes in those circumstances?

She returned my stare. Her dark eyes were moist. 'Please,' she mouthed.

'Okay,' I said.

The police had been called, including a detective from the nearest town. He didn't waste much time before interviewing us all, in the manager's office. I was first.

The detective's name was Sergeant O'Leary. He was a middle-aged man with a policeman's moustache, wearing a brown suit, and I could see the rim of a black sweater under the collar of his white shirt. His tie was brown with grey stripes, right out of the seventies. He was business-like, and asked pointed questions in a distinctive accent, New Hampshire, presumably. He asked me about my movements, about the details of my run that morning, and about what I knew of Harald and the other candidates. I told him what I could, although I missed out my suspicions about Harald and Manola. It was hard to concentrate on his questions. The reality of the murder hadn't sunk into my exhausted, jet-lagged brain. Apparently Harald's body had been found near the lake. His head had been bludgeoned with a rock.

Something was nagging at my mind. As I left the manager's office, I paused. 'Haven't I seen you somewhere before?'

O'Leary snorted. 'I doubt it, sir. I took a vacation to London with the kids a few years ago, but it's pretty unlikely we met then.'

'No,' I said. 'Of course not.' But there *was* something. It was as much his mannerisms, that snort for example, as anything else. As you know, I never forget a face, or a name. But I couldn't place him.

We waited in stunned silence as everyone was interviewed. Manola disappeared to her room as soon as her interview was finished. Trent made an attempt at light-hearted comments to break the tension, but failed and disappeared too. Myself, Charlie Cameron the Canadian, and Phil Riviani, a balding, overweight analyst who had been with the Houston office for fifteen years, waited in silence. The case was forgotten. I tried to go for a walk by the lake, but a uniformed policeman barred my way.

Eventually, Bill appeared, followed by Steve Goldberg, who had fetched Manola and Trent from their cabins. Manola's eyes were rimmed red. Bill perched on the dining-room table and addressed us grimly.

'This is clearly the worst day in our firm's history,' he began. 'Harald was a great guy, he would have made a terrific partner, and we all miss him. We will all need time to mourn him in our own way. But for now, we have something very serious to consider. I have been speaking with Sergeant O'Leary, and he is of the strong opinion that whoever murdered Harald was staying at the camp. It snowed in the middle of last night and there are no fresh tracks anywhere leading in here. Of course, this suggests that the murderer could have been one of the staff at the camp, and the police are questioning them very closely as we speak. But, and I hate to say this . . .' he paused and looked regretfully at each of our faces, 'it is most likely that Harald's killer is one of us. Or rather, one of you.'

He waited for our reaction. There wasn't one for several seconds, before Charlie Cameron spoke. 'You can't be serious,' he said.

Bill shrugged. 'I find it very hard to accept, myself, but there is no other conclusion.'

'It doesn't make sense,' I said.

'Sergeant O'Leary thinks it does,' Bill said. 'But I have every confidence in the loyalty and integrity of our people. Before he takes you all off to the nearest police station, I have persuaded him to allow you an hour to discuss it amongst yourselves. You've all worked together in the past, I'm sure you can figure out which one of you is responsible. You have an hour.'

With that, he was gone.

He left the rest of us, the five of us, staring at each other. It was an extraordinary situation, totally disorienting. Here we were, miles from anywhere, dealing with the surreal. I couldn't accept it. 'This is all bollocks,' I said. 'None of us killed Harald.'

'No,' said Phil Riviani. 'None of us can have done. It must have been an outsider.'

Charlie Cameron nodded. Trent and Manola were motionless.

'So what do we do?' Phil said.

'We wait an hour and then talk to the police again,' I replied.

'I guess so,' said Phil.

We looked at each other in silence. The dining room must have been a recent addition to the lodge. It had a high-vaulted ceiling and big picture windows, giving a view of the lake, sunshine glaring white off its flat snowy surface. There were no signs of human habitation. Framed by the window, the winter landscape looked like something out of a Christmas card, not the scene of a murder.

'You went for a run this morning,' said Trent to me.

'As did you. So what?' I said.

'I didn't kill him.'

'And neither did I.'

'What did the police say to you?' Charlie Cameron asked me, carefully.

'They asked me about my run. Whether I saw anything. Whether I knew any reason why any of us would want to kill Harald.'

'And what did you say?' Charlie asked.

'That I didn't. Why?'

'Well, when the police spoke to me, most of the interview was about you. They wanted to know all about your background, your ambitions, about your time working with Harald in London.'

'They asked if I knew that you had once threatened to kill Harald,' Phil said.

'What! Harald and I got on well. I never threatened him.'

'Until Bill told us that Harald was in pole position for partnership, you were the favourite,' Trent said. 'O'Leary asked me lots of questions about your desire to become a partner.'

I looked around the assembled group. They were puzzled, doubtful, but they were also suspicious. I could feel it in the air. All except Manola who was staring blankly ahead of her, blinking.

'This is ridiculous,' I said. 'I didn't kill him. None of us killed him.'

'Somebody did,' said Charlie Cameron in a reasonable tone. There was silence. Charlie, Phil and Trent all stared at me.

'I know who killed Harald,' Manola said in a whisper so low I wasn't sure I had heard it. She was rocking backward and forward in her chair. Her face was red, and her expression tight as a drum, as if she were struggling to hold in a mighty force. 'Harald and I had a relationship. We were engaged, actually.' She held up her left hand, revealing a cluster of diamonds around her finger. 'Of course we had to keep it secret. I put his ring on when I went to my room just now.'

'I didn't know,' said Charlie. He and Phil looked completely surprised. Trent slouched back in his chair. His lips weren't actually smiling, but he seemed, well, satisfied.

'I'm sorry, Manola,' I said.

She ignored me and took a deep breath. 'They say it's stupid to enter into a relationship with someone at work. In the case of Harald I don't regret it for a moment, he was a wonderful man, but sometimes they are right.' She sniffed. 'What was stupid was the night I spent with Trent. It was eighteen months ago, before Harald. We were on a trip to Angola, we'd had a few too many drinks in the hotel bar. It was an awful mistake as I told Trent right afterwards. But he wouldn't accept it.'

'Are you saying I killed Harald?' Trent said with scorn.

'You were jealous. You were insanely, stupidly jealous, especially when you realised that Harald and I were having a relationship and that that relationship was serious.'

'I was just kidding,' said Trent, looking uncomfortable.

'You stalked me! You followed us when we went out on dates. You called me up in the middle of the night. You sent me flowers, letters. You know you did all that, Trent.'

Now it was Trent's turn to blush.

'But there was no need to kill him,' Manola's voice was speeding up. She began to shake. 'What did you think would happen when he was dead? Did you think I would fall into your arms, my fiancé's killer? Did you think I would ever speak to you again?'

'Hey, I didn't kill him!' Trent protested.

Manola was on her feet. 'Of course you killed him! Peter didn't, why would Peter do something like that? But he saw you out running by the lake, didn't he? You killed him. You're a murderer, Trent!'

She was screaming now, her face red, spittle flying from her lips. She launched into a tirade of Spanish, and lunged towards him. I stood up and took her by the arm. 'It's okay, Manola,' I tried to say. 'It's okay.'

'It's not okay, Peter,' she said, but she was sobbing. 'I've got to get out of here. I can't stand being in the room with him.'

'Here, I'll take you back to your cabin,' I said. I led her out of the dining room. The policeman guarding the door was about to stop her, but I glared at him. He stepped out of our way. I took her to her room and left her there, promising I would be back in a few minutes.

As I walked back to the lodge I wondered what to do. I had no doubt that Manola was right, that Trent was jealous of her affair with Harald. But had he killed him? It just seemed so absurd, so unreal. The whole thing seemed unreal.

I saw the policeman waiting by the door. He was tall and nervous; Manola's hysterics had clearly shaken him. He didn't look like a country policeman at all. He was soft, no tough guy. I stared at him. A policeman, even in rural New Hampshire, should be able to handle angry women better than he had. Suddenly I knew where I had seen Sergeant O'Leary before.

'Where's your squad car?' I asked the policeman.

'Out back,' he said.

'I'm going to see it,' I said. 'And I'm going to take a look at where Harald was killed.' I turned towards the path around the side of the building.

'I'm afraid I can't let you do that, sir,' he said, stepping in front of me.

'How can you stop me?'

'I can restrain you, sir. I'm a policeman.'

'Are you quite sure about that?' I said.

I burst into the manager's office. Bill, 'Sergeant O'Leary' and Steve Goldberg were sitting watching a small video screen on which was a view of a heated discussion between Trent, Phil and Charlie.

Bill turned around, and smiled when he saw me. 'Well, well, well. I thought if anyone figured it out it would be you. How did you do it?'

'You're an actor, aren't you?' I said to the man in the bad suit. 'You had a bit part in *The West Wing* a few years ago.'

'You remembered that?' said O'Leary. 'I'm impressed. No one ever recognises me from that. I was only in one episode.'

'Where's Harald?' I asked.

'He's fine,' Bill said. 'He's at the motel in town. We whisked him away in the middle of the night. He has no idea what's going on here. Poor fellow never was on the partnership track, but I needed a fall guy to play the favourite.'

'What the hell are you doing?' I demanded, making no attempt to hide my anger.

'Calm down, Peter,' Bill said, giving me his warmest grin. 'This was the ultimate partnership test. We wanted you to be the chief suspect, and I must say you handled it pretty well. But that affair between Manola and Harald was quite unexpected. I wouldn't have thought he was her type. And I've learned a lot about Trent as well.'

'Did you see what you did to her?' I demanded.

'Manola has a tendency to lose her cool; that's really her biggest weakness. She'll be fine this afternoon once she knows Harald is okay. And she'll be laughing about it next week.'

'I don't think so,' I said. 'I really don't think so.'

'My God, look!' We both turned to see Steve Goldberg pointing to the video screen. It was a good picture, in colour. Manola was walking towards Trent, her back to the camera. Behind her back she was clutching a long carving knife from the ham platter. Trent hadn't seen it yet, his expression was a mixture of embarrassment and complacency.

I ran for the door and sprinted across the hallway to the dining room. And then I heard Trent scream.

'Whew,' I said, when Peter had finished.

'Are you still going to join Labouchere?' he said.

I shook my head. 'So, that's why you quit, then?'

'Yes. As did Harald, and Manola, of course. They split up.'

'Understandable, I suppose. Did she actually kill Trent?'

'Yes. It was covered up. It required all Bill Labouchere's considerable organisational skills and influence. We all felt complicit so we all helped. We thought Manola had suffered extreme provocation, but we couldn't be sure the courts would see it that way. In my opinion it was Bill who really killed Trent.'

'But Labouchere Associates is still going strong?'

'Going from strength to strength. The others stayed on as if nothing had happened. Charlie Cameron was even made a partner. No one mentions Lake Lenatonka. Ever.' Then Peter frowned. He had seen someone over my shoulder. 'Oh Christ,' he said. 'I forgot we arranged to meet here. For God's sake, don't mention any of this, will you?'

'No, of course not,' I said. I turned to see who Peter had spotted. Coming towards us was a dark-haired woman in an expensive low-cut cream suit and high heels. She was drop-dead gorgeous and the noise level in the bar dropped as every man turned to watch her make her way across to us.

She smiled when she saw Peter, a wide warm smile and kissed him quickly on the lips. Peter swallowed. 'Mike, I don't think you've met my wife, have you?'

She turned her smile to me. 'Hi,' she said, in an American accent. 'I'm Manola. I've heard so much about you.'

'Likewise,' I said. 'Likewise.'

A TOOTHBRUSH

H.R.F. Keating

Henry Tailor, assistant inspector in the Small Branches Division of mighty H.J. Manifold's, arrived late at his house in sweetly suburban Harrow-on-the-Hill. Victim of the hospitality of the over-anxious manager of the Bedford branch, he had missed, by a minute, his train back. He had had then to sit for a whole hour in the station waiting room, thinking how much nicer it would be to be looking down at his Alice, his quiet little wife of three years, an early-to-bedder if ever there was, as she lay innocently asleep.

Home at last, totally weary, when he did stand there beside her he found himself in a dilemma. Go to the bathroom and get rid of any trace of alcohol on his breath – Alice hated it – by quickly brushing his teeth? Or, forgetting his toothbrush, the green one, side by side in the mug with Alice's pink one, put his clothes neatly on his chair, slip his pyjamas from under his pillow and just slide in beside her as she slept on?

Modest intake of wine still coursing through his veins, he finally decided. Be a devil. Alice will never know.

But next morning, leaving Alice still snugly there for her few extra minutes, as he stepped into the bathroom he saw at once, in the familiar scratched blue plastic mug on the shelf above the basin, a totally alien toothbrush.

*   *   *

29

It came as a shock. As if . . . As if, he was to say after-wards, it had been left there by a real alien, a little man from Mars. In a moment, of course, various explanations occurred to him, likely or unlikely. The likeliest – he could not even think the brush might belong to someone Alice had invited in – was that she had bought herself a new one. But that, in fact, was not at all likely. For one thing he was almost sure she had acquired her pink-handled brush only a month or so ago – she had always said it was better to have a different colour from his – and in any case the alien brush was not at all like anything Alice would ever buy.

No, this brush, the alien one, was, well – alien. It had a very broad long white handle, looking something like a spatula. Its head, too, was large, larger than that on any toothbrush he had ever seen, and its bristles, thick, and somehow aggressive, were noticeably longer than the ones on Alice's or his own.

He wanted, and did not want, to touch it, to pick the thing up and examine it more carefully. But in the end, after taking his shower, thinking hard the while, all he did was delicately to extract his green brush from the scratched old mug, use it, more hastily than usual, and slip it back into the mug close beside Alice's, almost touching in fact. Then, standing rather far back from the mirror, he started his razor buzzing.

But, dressing finished, just as Alice stirred he made a sudden dash into the bathroom again and – he did not really know why – snatched up the alien thing, stood for just one moment looking at it, and then stuffed it – it was quite dry – into the inner pocket of his jacket next to his wallet.

Sitting in the kitchen over his two quick cups of tea and one thick slice of toast and marmalade, with Alice opposite in her pink-roses housecoat – her library job did not start till ten – he managed to slant his tentative inquiries about how she had spent the time while he had been in Bedford into the subject of shopping. Then, when this produced nothing, he asked whether she had remembered to renew . . . Not, absolutely not, her quite new toothbrush but, randomly hit on, the half-empty jar of marmalade.

'No,' Alice said, in her usual neatly efficient manner, 'if we're careful we won't need more till we go for the big shop on Saturday.'

Henry would have liked to have tried some other approach. Each time he thought about that wide, gleaming white toothbrush he had seen planted between the two of theirs in the mug, he felt a dart of disquiet. But time was getting on, and he was never, except when there was a strike on the Underground, late for work.

So he swallowed the last of his tea, folded his napkin, put it in its ring and went to collect his briefcase from its place in the hall, calling out his customary 'Goodbye, darling, see you about six.'

Then, as he closed the hall door, as usual firmly, a new thought struck him.

He hauled his key from his trouser pocket, the right-hand one of course, handkerchief always in the left, slid it into the Yale, opened the door, and, shouting out the first thing that came to mind, 'Forgotten something', he thrust his head into the sitting room, glanced rapidly round – windows all intact, latches in place – before running upstairs, heedless now of any noise he might make, and taking an equally quick survey of the windows there.

Yes, each one properly closed, as Alice always made sure they were before going to bed. So, how . . .? But no time to think about that now.

'Got it,' he called out (*What can I say* it *is, if Alice* . . .?)

and in a minute he was striding down the road towards the station, briefcase swinging from his hand.

At his desk in Manifold House he found it hard to concentrate on his report on the Bedford branch. The thought of the alien toothbrush kept flicking up in his mind, like a colour TV ad during an old black-and-white film, momentarily startling and then back to the monotone world of yesteryear. But the puzzle of that mysterious arrival in the scratched old plastic mug seemed to be without any practical answer. Earlier in the train, when in putting his wallet back after tucking his travel card away he had just touched it, he had felt so dazed he had been unable to bring his mind to consider it at all. But now, for minutes-long spells, he found himself doing nothing but grinding and grinding away at the out-of-this-world puzzle.

But is it really out-of-this-world, he asked himself almost every other time the image of the over-large white toothbrush entered his head. Can it be? Can my house, our own little house, have actually been invaded by Martians? By toothbrush-using Martians? No, ridiculous. Impossible. But then had Alice, for some unfathomable reason, really gone out and bought such a strange object? As totally unlikely.

Once even he went to the toilets and, in a safely locked cubicle, took out the monster brush and peered and peered at it. But no enlightenment came. A burglar? A burglar, while sleepy Alice slept and slept? No. All the windows had been shut and intact, and no sign either of the back door or the front having been forced. And, anyhow, why should a burglar do no more than just put that extraordinary object into the mug?

So did this thing in my hands, he thought, somehow just materialise, there where I saw it as I stepped into the bathroom? Where I snatched it up before Alice could see it? For heaven's sake, science fiction is fiction, pure fiction, and I, Henry Tailor, am real. As real as— As this toothbrush I'm staring at.

Quickly he put it back in his jacket pocket – what if someone spots it, asks questions? – and as soon as he was at his desk he surreptitiously transferred it to his briefcase. Then, for the first time ever, he used its tinny little key.

At a late stage of the afternoon he recognised that he had managed to scrabble together some sort of a report on the Bedford branch. Muddled though it was, he thought in a moment of inner truth, it would get much the same reception up above as the properly thorough ones he prided himself on submitting. Still, putting it in the internal post – H.J. Manifold's disapproved of inter-office e-mailing – he felt a small surge of relief. And with that came an idea.

Is there perhaps, here in the building, some disinterested outsider I could talk to about all this? At once then, with a sudden bad-taste gulp, he realised that *all this* meant, in the deepest recesses of his mind, the possibility that— That the alien toothbrush had somehow been there in the bathroom because of Alice. Because Alice really had the lover he had dismissed from his mind almost before the thought had entered his head? But, no, no, no. That was just not possible, not my Alice.

So shall I, at five o'clock, look out for Peter Crossley-Smith from Major Branches – he'd be the one – and suggest a quick drink? I could still be home by *about six*. I've done it before. I did it when, deciding for once to go out with two or three of 'the boys', I met Peter. Old Five Wives, as they call him, sometimes to his face. When he invariably replies, with that neighing laugh of his, *Probably be Old Six Wives before I'm done.*

*   *   *

For once, as it turned out, Old Five Wives was not surrounded by any noisy departing slaves from the H.J. Manifold's mill. Henry was able to fall into step beside him and, after he had suggested the statutory 'quick pint', managed even to say there was something he particularly wanted to discuss, 'a sort of, well, private matter, so perhaps we could go somewhere different for a change.'

'Touch of the naughties, is it?' Five Wives, propped at the unfamiliar bar, immediately asked.

'Oh. No, no. No, nothing of that sort. I'm a happily married . . . Well, no, it's something a bit odd actually.'

'Say on, old chap, say on. I must admit I've never quite seen you as an entrant in the Naughty Stakes. Unlike, alas, yours very truly.'

'No. No, I suppose not. But I do need— Well, I need sort of advice from someone. And you're— Well, you're what I think of as a man of the world.'

'The worldly ear is at your disposal. Tell.'

Henry, going down in the crowded lift at Manifold House, had fully rehearsed the story he would have to recount. So it was without too many apologies and back-trackings that he poured it all out.

And was rewarded.

'Yes. Odd. Pretty odd, I'll grant you that.'

Long swallow at the pint. Then a quick glance.

'Little lady having a touch of the wandering-eye syndrome? It goes either way, you know. Had some either-way trouble once myself, with Number Three actually.'

'No. I'm quite certain. Absolutely certain. Look, I've been married to Alice for three whole years, and—'

'Take your word for it, take your word for it. But I say, old fellow, you haven't been working a bit too hard lately?'

'Well, I like to think I'm a decently hard worker, but I don't believe—' Abruptly he straightened up on his bar-stool.

'You're not saying . . .? Listen, if you're thinking I may have gone bonkers and imagined it all, well, I can absolutely prove the whole business is absolutely, absolutely true. Look. Look.'

He dived for the briefcase, carefully placed between his stretched-out toes at the foot of his bar-stool, hoisted it up, found in his right-hand trouser pocket its little shiny key and took out the alien toothbrush.

Five Wives looked at it with almost as much disbelief as Henry had felt when he had found it plunged between the pink and the green brushes nestling in the familiar mug.

'And this morning you saw it, this thing, in your bathroom? And it wasn't there last night. That it?'

'Well, you've got it a bit wrong. I didn't, as it happens, go into the bathroom last night. I thought— Well, never mind, I didn't happen to go in there.'

'Not for a last pee?'

Henry made an effort to be man to man.

'No. We've got a toilet downstairs. Used that.'

Five Wives considered for a second or two.

'Well, old man,' he said, 'I must admit you've fairly got me stumped.'

Henry felt a tumbling-away of hope. He saw himself as an Antarctic explorer, ice-crusted glove slipping and slipping on the slithery rope holding him over a deathly deep crevasse.

'You can't— You can't suggest anything I ought to do, then?' he asked. 'Anything?'

'Well, frankly, no. Not unless you go to a private eye. Had to do that once meself. Over Number Three, matter of fact.'

'And was he helpful, the chap you went to? I mean, well, private detectives are jolly expensive, aren't they?'

'Not this one, actually. Fellow in a small way, very small way. And was he helpful? Well, if you call being helpful finding out what I'd already pretty well guessed about

Number Three, then, yes, he was a help. Though I had to divorce her, of course. Things usually other way round. But life's full of surprises.'

So it was that Henry Tailor found himself next Saturday in West London walking along tourist-crowded Queensway peering into narrow doorways between its bright and bouncy shops. He was looking for a small sign just inside one of them, distracted by a feeling that he had forgotten what reason he had given Alice for having to go up to work.

But at last, when he had almost begun to think Five Wives' private eye was every bit as imaginary as the alien toothbrush – only that wasn't imaginary at all – he saw between a drop-in dry cleaner's and an electrical goods shop the discreet notice he was looking for.

TOP Investigations. Please ring and walk up.

His finger on the bell-push was so tentative it might not have produced any buzz at all. But it did. The sound came down the narrow flight of stairs in front of him, unmistakably. So he felt he had to *walk up*.

The door at the top, pale wood with a peep-hole in its centre, opened as he reached the little patch of landing. A pale girl, looking about sixteen, blonde hair caught up at the back with a rubber band, gave him an incurious look.

'Mr Pepper's free at the moment,' she said. 'You can go straight in.'

But he paused for an instant before stepping forward.

I'm visiting a private eye, he thought. Here I am, Henry Tailor, and I'm about to hire a private eye. Or I may be. If . . . If he can suggest there's anything to do about— About the alien toothbrush.

He swallowed, and advanced on the inner door, its reeded glass panel inscribed in black *Mr Thomas Pepper*. He put his hand – it was suddenly sweaty – on the knob, twisted, found he had no purchase, tightened his grip, twisted again and the door swung so wide that he almost stumbled inside.

Behind a small desk – the room itself was small enough – a man rose to greet him, hand held out. He did not look at all like the private eye Henry had envisaged. Somehow it was impossible to think of that extended hand as holding a gun or that in the bottom drawer of that desk there would be a bottle of bourbon, or even of Scotch. Red-faced, Thomas Pepper was, if not actually fat, certainly a very solid shape. But, somehow again, not a shape adapted to sudden action. His shoulders were, plainly, stooped and his brown suit looked as if it was worn unchanged day after day.

'Tom Pepper, at your service. Tom Pepper, *TP*, where I got *TOP Investigations* from. My little joke. Should have been *TP Investigations*, but couldn't resist that extra O. Make it sound big. Ah, well . . .'

'Oh, yes. Yes.' Henry cleared his throat. 'Look, there's – there's something . . .'

'Here, take a pew. Take the pew, only one there is. And tell me all about it, beginning—' He drew a virgin-white pad towards himself— 'with the name.'

It was all, abruptly, cosy. A cosy atmosphere.

Henry sat in the chair in front of the desk, a comfortably padded one, and having given his name and spelt out that always difficult $T - A - I - L - O - R$, not $T - A - Y$, once again produced the story of the alien toothbrush. In full detail.

He saw, when he had come to the end, that Tom Pepper was as baffled as he had been himself, even turning to the computer at the corner of the desk and peering at it with a look of hopelessly hopeful expectation.

'Yes,' he said at last. 'Wonderful things, computers. They never made enough use of 'em when I was in the Force, spent all their time feeding in information and not enough getting information out. No, this little feller's what I call the real Policeman's Friend, not the thing used to be in your trousers case you were taken short out on the beat.'

He gave the keyboard at his elbow a little tap of gratitude.

'Know what I found out on it the other day? Just who the original Tom Pepper was. Out of curiosity, tapped in me own name. Found that, back in the 1800s, Tom Pepper was a champion liar. He was a sailor, and he drowned and, natch, went to Hell. And, do you know, he told so many lies down there that in the end they had to kick him out. Out of Hell. My ancestor. But, don't you worry, this Tom Pepper's no liar. Well, only sometimes. Interests of truth.'

Henry began to think his trip up to Queensway was going to be a waste of time. But Tom Pepper's next remark gave him a little burst of hope.

'Yes, but get down to it. What you've told me's interesting. Very. Make a nice case. Beats standing in the rain, erring wife, wandering daughter, or, come to that, lying in the dust putting a bug under a bed. You got that toothbrush here?'

'No. No, I haven't. Actually, it's locked in my briefcase, and I didn't bring that with me.'

'Doesn't matter,' Tom Pepper said comfortably. 'See, way I work, it's bit of a chat with the client first, 'specially with a matrimonial, and then ask 'em to come in again, with the photos or whatever. And, of course, initial fees. Gives 'em time to change their mind. Often do, the ladies. No skin off my nose. Client who doesn't really want to be one, nothing but a pain in the whatsit. Neck.'

But in Henry's mind a more immediate anxiety had been set up.

'Er – the fee?' he said. 'I mean . . . Well, how much will that be?'

'Right. Down to business. Best way. So, initial's two hundred and fifty.'

He must have seen the look on Henry's face. He was watching him keenly enough.

'But that's matrimonials. Or missing persons. Your case? Well, make it a straight two hundred. View of the interest.'

'Yes, I see. But – But, well, how much will it be after that?'

'Hard to say, hard to say. Depends how much work there turns out to be. I charge by the hour. So, might come a bit pricey. Other hand, if all I do is sit here poking about on the Net, could be a lot cheaper. Here's my little printed note. Take it away. Have a ponder. Then give me a tinkle. Or not.'

Henry had waited till the following Saturday – 'Quite a rush on at Manifold House,' he told Alice – but he arrived at the cramped little office in Queensway at exactly ten a.m., with in his wallet pocket the alien toothbrush and ten carefully folded twenty-pound notes.

Sitting once more in front of Tom Pepper, he thrust them out.

There. Done it.

Tom slipped the bundle into the drawer in front of him.

'So, we're on,' he said. 'Mystery of the missing toothbrush. Or, come to think of it, mystery of the anything-but-missing toothbrush. You got it with you this time?'

Henry handed it across.

'Right. Your dabs all over of course, and no doubt your pal's, Mr Crossley-Smith. Very nice sort of client, Mr Smith. So what've we got?'

A long scrutiny.

'Yes. Useful sort of name here. Gold letters. *The Aristocrat*. Tells us something.'

Henry, who had taken little notice of the flowing golden letters, could not think what they could tell anybody.

'America,' Tom Pepper said. 'Bet a shilling. You ever see anybody this country calling a toothbrush *The Aristocrat*? No, it's only over there they fancy aristocracy. Haven't got any of their own, that's why.'

Henry was impressed. A little progress. Straight away.

Then he saw Tom Pepper looking at him.

'You want to go on with this, son? Because you're in trouble. You know that?'

'But – But why? I mean, just because that funny-looking toothbrush somehow got into the mug in our bathroom, surely it can't mean anything . . . Anything, well, serious?'

'Oh, but it does. If you go on with this, let me tell you, something mucky'll come your way. Can smell it. Still, if you don't go on, something mucky'll still turn up. You'd better believe that.'

What *mucky*? Henry thought. How could anything mucky be happening to me?

And then the idea of what might be mucky tickled again at a corner of his mind. But impossible. Impossible.

He sat forward in Tom Pepper's comfortable client's chair.

'Look,' he said with a touch of real ferocity, 'how do I know I can trust you, Mr Pepper?'

Tom Pepper gave a hint of a smile.

He sat back then and pulled open the drawer in front of him. From it he took the little wad of twenties Henry had so carefully folded together and slapped it down on the desk.

'That's why,' he said.

And then, somehow, Henry found he had taken his decision.

'Yes,' he said. 'Yes, Mr Pepper, I do want to go on with it. And I'll pay anything more there is. I'll pay, whatever it takes.'

For the third Saturday running Henry told Alice that there was *a rush on at Manifold House*. Luckily, she always left matters concerning his work altogether to him, and simply said she could manage to do the big shop quite nicely on her own this week. So for a third time he made his way along the crowded Queensway pavement, thinking vaguely what a good thing it was that Alice liked nothing better than being at home – no gallivanting, no going out at nights – until he came to that discreet sign, *TOP Investigations*. In the cramped little office Tom Pepper, in the same old brown suit, was sitting there, computer glowing beside him, with the toothbrush lying on the battered green-leather surface of the desk. Smooth, long and brightly white, its thick bristles projecting arrogantly upwards. More alien than ever.

'Sit down, Mr Tailor. Or shall I say Henry? Better be first names, news I've got for you.'

Murmuring polite agreement to *Henry*, he found in his head an insistent question. *What sort of news? What sort? What?*

But, when he was told, he found himself as much puzzled as ever.

'You ever heard of a pop group called The Sixth?'

'A pop group? I – I'm afraid we don't ever listen to that sort of music at home. I don't really know anything about it. I mean, I've heard of the Beatles, of course. But . . .'

'You not on the Internet?'

'Well, no. I can get it at the office. Well, I could, if I wanted to, I suppose. But, no, I'm not – er – connected at home.'

'Pity. As I was saying the other day – correct me if I'm wrong – there's a lot can be found out on the Net. Fr'instance, you can get to know the whole history of The Sixth, press enough keys.'

'But – But why should you want to know anything like that? I don't understand.'

'Well, let me tell you a bit, then perhaps you'll begin to see what I'm getting at. Right, there was this little lot of schoolboys up in Aylesbury—'

'Aylesbury?' Henry could not stop himself breaking in. 'That's where my Alice was born and brought up.'

'So she was, so she was. Found that on the old Net. Births, marriages and deaths. Poked around some more. And bingo.'

Henry sat without making any comment. Dim thoughts were rolling now in the deepest recesses of his mind. Dim, dark thoughts.

'Right, The Sixth,' Tom Pepper went on. 'Name those school kids gave themselves – all in the sixth form, Aylesbury Grammar – when they began with their guitars and that. Then they got themselves a manager and the act took off. Suppose the boys looked nice and cuddly, and in no time they'd got fans galore and pots of money. Till all of a sudden the manager quit, and they folded.'

'But how . . .?' Henry ventured, as much as anything to fight down those dim, dark, whirling fog masses. 'Why does all this have anything to do with that toothbrush there?'

'Ask the Net. And what d'you find? *The Sixth Make Their Come-back*. Harrow Town Hall. Three Tuesdays back.'

The dark rolling clouds seemed suddenly to solidify in Henry's head.

'But that was when I went up to Bedford,' he said.

'So it was. Funny thing that, ain't it? Think you told me when you spoke to your little Alice at breakfast next morning, trying to see if she knew anything about this toothbrush here, she let you believe she'd done nothing out of the ordinary that day. But you know what my old friend the Net said? Ticket was bought for that concert in the name of Alice Tailor.'

Henry heard in his head, clearly as clearly, Old Five

Wives' voice saying, *Touch of the wandering-eye syndrome. It goes either way, you know.*

Tom Pepper broke in. 'Now what did I tell you? Just exactly what? Only one ticket for that concert, not two. So, don't you get to thinking more than the evidence warrants.'

'But if— If she isn't— Wasn't— If . . . No, you're trying to make me believe she— No, right, I'm calling all this off. I no longer require your services. How— How much do I owe you?'

'Oh, forget that. What's an hour or two on the Internet?'

'Then give me back that toothbrush, and— And— And—'

'Okay. Yours after all. Found in your house. In that mug. Yours, if it isn't someone else's.'

Snatching the gleaming white object, Henry turned for the door.

'No,' Tom Pepper said. 'No, can't let you go like that.'

He looked about him as if for help, even giving a glance to the glowing but blank screen beside him.

Henry had his hand on the door-knob. Once again it was clammy with sudden sweat. He twisted and slid and twisted again.

'Look,' Tom Pepper said, 'you're afloat on a dangerous sea, my lad. You've no idea how dangerous. Believe this all-alive-o Tom Pepper right in front of you, he's not lying.'

Henry got the door open.

He saw that in his left hand he was still clutching the white toothbrush, *The Aristocrat*. It seemed to be – if this could be so – glowing with evil alien energy.

He turned and ran down the narrow stairs, out into bustling Queensway, faintly hearing Tom Pepper still calling, 'Oh, come back, come back. There's more.'

*   *   *

At home, alien toothbrush eventually shoved into inner pocket, Henry was greeted by Alice, demure in pale yellow cardigan.

'Darling, that's nice. I thought you wouldn't be back for ages.'

Again Henry heard Old Five Wives' neighing voice. *It goes either way, you know.*

The wandering-eye syndrome.

And then, though he had vowed and vowed that he never would, he yanked the alien toothbrush from his pocket and thrust it under Alice's pretty, upturned nose.

'Tell me what this is,' he shouted. 'Tell me how it got to be in our toothmug, in our bathroom.'

The colour left Alice's cheeks, as if it had never been there.

'In our bathroom?' she said, voice barely audible. 'You found it there?'

'I did. And I strongly suspect you knew it was there all the time.'

'No.' She swallowed fiercely. 'Darling, I never had any idea it was there. He— He must have . . . While I was at the concert, The Sixth's come-back one. He must have come over from America for that. He was their manager originally. So it must have been him who put that ticket through the letter-box. I thought it was one of the girls at work. I told them once my schoolgirl dream about The Sixth.'

'But you went? Went to that concert?' he said, almost snarled.

'Well, yes, I did. I did. You were up in Bedford, and I thought suddenly I'd like to see them, see if they were the same. And they weren't. They were awful. But while I was out of the house he must have . . . But how did he know that I lived . . .? No, he must have just seen me in the street. Perhaps on Saturday, the big shop.'

She came to a choked halt. Then, trembling, she began again.

'Oh, Henry, I never could tell you about – about – about the terrible thing he did to me, when I'd only just finished school. That summer. Why he suddenly had to leave for America.'

Henry found then that his anger and his suspicions had gone. Alice's utter distress had swept them away. A swirl of dust before a blast of clean wind.

'No, darling,' he said. 'You didn't tell—'

Then he realised that behind him the telephone had been ringing and ringing.

It could be Tom Pepper, he thought, though he could not have said why he felt it.

He snatched up the receiver.

'Hello, hello?'

'Well now, if that ain't the hubby,' said a treacly voice, strongly American-accented. 'Okay, you can give little Alice a message. From Curtiss Boyer. Just say, I left my toothbrush while she was at the concert, and when you're away on one of your Tuesday trips, Mr Hubby – I've researched you, old buddy – I'll drop by and collect.'

Swindon was next on Henry's Tuesday list. He left to go there, deciding he would not relay that message from Curtiss Boyer, even though Alice had told him how that summer long ago, in the absence from home of her parents, he had bullied her into letting him stay. But, having gone to the point of actually catching a Swindon train, in case he was being kept under observation, he got off as soon as he could – the train, unfortunately, was nonstop to Chippenham – and hurryingly returned.

At home he told Alice why he was there. Tearfully, she thanked him.

'But – but if he comes, what are you going to do?' she said. 'You'd have to have a gun to stop that brute.'

'I wouldn't dare use a gun, even if I did have one. I wouldn't actually properly know how.'

'But then, darling . . .?'

'No, we'll just have to wait and see. He may not come, you know. He may have just wanted to scare you by leaving one of those toothbrushes of his.'

'I suppose so, but . . .'

'Well, we'll see. At least I'm here with you.'

So they waited. They were too tense when it came to supper time even to think of eating anything.

Darkness fell, and they sat on, where they were in their usual armchairs, one on either side of the mute telly.

'I don't think we'll even have the News,' Henry said at last, dry-mouthed.

'No. No, we must be ready to hear the least sound.'

That least sound came a little later. A slight but unmistakable noise from the front door. Henry knew at once exactly what it was.

I must have read about it somewhere, he thought. It's the faint scratching made by a thin plastic card being forced into the crack between door and jamb and worked up and down to push back the tongue of the lock. But why ever didn't I think of putting the snib down? Because, I suppose, we never do that. We never have. That must be how, before, he . . .

'It's him,' Alice breathed, taut with anxiety.

It was.

He was there just beyond the door, plain to see in the light of the hall. Slab-faced, bulkily tall, a somehow American buff-coloured raincoat hanging from his shoulders. He glared into the darkened room. Then gave a little jerk back.

'Hey, it's Mr Hubby. Life's full of surprises, I guess.'

But, beyond that, he did not seem in any way put out.

He took an idle step forward towards Alice, crammed against the back of her chair as if she was pasted to it.

'You wanna watch, Mr Hubby?'

Henry found he had risen up from his chair, even while he still felt he was fixed as fast into it as Alice was into hers.

He took three quaking strides and put himself between her and the menacing intruder.

Who moved both his arms towards him in a scooping gesture, as if he intended to lift this air-light object out of the way. But Henry's hand dived into his inner pocket, and brought out that big, white, spatula-like toothbrush.

'Yours, I believe,' he said, however creakingly. 'Kindly take it and go.'

Curtiss Boyer laughed. A wide, mouth-open guffaw.

And Henry struck.

He sent the alien toothbrush shooting forward straight into that softly red, yawning crater.

With a howl of rage and pain, Curtiss Boyer staggered back.

But he was not quelled for long.

His eyes widened in fury. Or perhaps in delight.

'Okay,' he said. 'Little man, you've asked for it.'

One lunging step forwards.

And from behind came an authoritative voice.

'Stop just where you are. You're under arrest. Citizen's arrest.'

A burly, brown-suited figure stepped quickly in, took an elbow in a holdfast grip.

'Caught up with you on the Net,' he said. 'Policeman's Friend. Not that I'm a proper copper any more. Still, mate of mine from those days is on his way. DI now. Make everything regular. Oh, and, Henry, you'd better put that toothbrush somewhere safe. Be needed in evidence.'

THE SUN, THE MOON
AND THE STARS

John Harvey

Eileen had done everything she could to change his mind. 'Michael,' she'd said, 'anywhere else, okay? Anywhere but there.' Michael Sandler, not his real name, not even close. But in the end she'd caved in, just as he'd known she would.

Thirty-three by not so many months and going nowhere; thirty-three, though she was still only owning up to twenty-nine.

When he'd met her she'd been a receptionist in a car showroom south of Sheffield, something she'd blagged her way into and held down for the best part of a year; fine until the head of sales had somehow got a whiff of her past employment, some potential customer who'd seen her stripping somewhere most likely, and tried wedging his podgy fingers up inside her skirt one evening late. Eileen had kneed him in the balls, then hit him with a solid glass ashtray high across the face, close to taking out an eye. She hadn't bothered waiting for her cards. She'd been managing a sauna, close to the city centre, when Michael had found her. In at seven, check the towels, make sure the plastic had been wiped down, bottles of massage oil topped up, the come washed from the walls; once the girls arrived, first shift, ready to catch the early punters on their way to work, she'd examine their hands, ensure they'd trimmed their nails;

uniforms they took home and washed, brought back next day clean as new or she'd want the reason why.

'Come on,' Michael had said, 'fifty minutes down the motorway. It's not as if I'm asking you to fucking emigrate.' Emigration might have been easier. She had memories of Nottingham and none of them good. But then, looking round at the tatty travel posters and old centrefolds from *Playboy* on the walls, he'd added, 'What? Worried a move might be bad for your career?'

It hadn't taken her long to pack her bags, turn over the keys. Fifty minutes on the motorway. A house like a barn, a palace, real paintings on the walls.

When he came home earlier than usual one afternoon and found her sitting in the kitchen, polishing the silver while she watched *Richard and Judy* on the small TV, he snatched the cloth from her hands. 'There's people paid for that, not you.'

'It's something to do.'

His nostrils flared. 'You want something to do, go down the gym. Go shopping. Read a fucking book.'

'Why?' she asked him later that night, turning towards him in their bed.

'Why what?'

'Why am I here?'

He didn't look at her. 'Because I'm tired of living on my own.'

He was sitting propped up against pillows, bare-chested, thumbing through the pages of a climbing magazine. Eileen couldn't imagine why: anything more than two flights of stairs and he took the lift.

The light from the lamp on his bedside table shone a filter of washed-out blue across the patterned quilt and the curtains stirred in the breeze from the opened window. One thing he insisted on, one of many, sleeping with at least one of the windows open.

'That's not enough,' Eileen said.

'What?'

'Enough of a reason for me being here. You being tired of living alone.'

After a long moment, he put down his magazine. 'It's not the reason, you know that.'

'Do I?' She leaned back as he turned towards her, his fingers touching her arm.

'I'm sorry about earlier,' he said. 'Snapping at you like that. It was stupid. Unnecessary.'

'It doesn't matter.'

'Yes, it does.'

His face was close to hers, too close for her to focus; there was a faint smell of brandy on his breath.

After they'd made love he lay on his side, watching her, watching her breathe.

'Don't,' she said.

'Don't what?'

'Don't stare. I hate it when you stare.' It reminded her of Terry, her ex, the way his eyes had followed her whenever he thought she wasn't looking; right up until the night he'd slipped the gun out from beneath the pillow and, just when she'd been certain he was going to take her life, had shot himself in the head.

'What else am I supposed to do?' Michael said.

'Go to sleep? Take a shower?' Her face relaxed into a smile. 'Read a fucking book?'

Michael grinned and reached across and kissed her. 'You want to know how much I love you?'

'Yeah, yeah.' Mocking.

After a little searching, he found a ball point in the bedside table drawer. Reaching for a magazine, he flicked through it till he came to a picture of the Matterhorn, outlined against the sky. 'Here,' he said, and quickly drew a hasty, childlike approximation of the sun, moon and stars around the summit. 'That's how much.'

Smiling, Eileen closed her eyes.

Resnick had spent the nub end of the evening in a pub off the A632 between Bolsover and Arkwright Town. Peter Waites and himself. From the outside it looked as if the place had been closed down months before and the interior was not a lot different. Resnick paced himself, supping halves, aware of having to drive back down, while Waites worked his way assiduously from pint to pint, much as he had when he'd been in his pomp and working at the coal face, twenty years before. Whenever it came to Waites' round, Resnick was careful to keep his wallet and his tongue well zipped, the man's pride buckled enough. He had lost his job in the wake of the miners' strike and not worked steady since.

'Not yet forty when they tossed me on the fuckin' scrap heap, Charlie. Me and a lot of others like me. Nigh on a thousand when that pit were closed and them pantywaist civil bloody servants chucking their hands up in the air on account they've found sixty new jobs. Bloody disgrace.' He snapped the filter from the end of his cigarette before lighting up.

'Lungs buggered enough already, Charlie. This'll not make ha'porth of difference, no matter what anyone says. Besides, long as I live long enough to see the last of that bloody woman and dance on her bloody grave, I don't give a sod.'

That bloody woman: Margaret Hilda Thatcher. In that company especially, no need to speak her name.

When they stepped outside the air bit cold. Over the carefully sculpted slag heap, now slick with grass, the moon hung bright and full. Of the twenty terraced houses in Peter Waites' street, fourteen were now boarded up.

'You'll not come in, Charlie?'

'Some other time.'

'Aye.' The two men shook hands.

'Look after yourself, Peter.'

'You, too.'

Resnick had first met the ex-miner when his son had joined the Notts force as a young PC and been stationed for a while at Canning Circus, under Resnick's wing. Now the boy was in Australia, married with kids, something in IT, and Resnick and Waites still kept in touch, the occasional pint, an odd Saturday at Bramhall Lane or down in Nottingham at the County ground, a friendship based on mutual respect and a sense of regret for days gone past.

Eileen would never be sure what woke her. The flap of the curtain as the window opened wider; the soft tread on the carpeted floor. Either way, when she opened her eyes there they were, two shrouded shapes beyond the foot of the bed. Beside her, Michael was already awake, pushing up on one elbow, hand reaching out towards the light.

'Leave it,' said a voice. The shapes beginning to flesh out, take on detail.

'We don't need the fucking light,' the shorter one said. A voice Eileen didn't recognise: one she would never forget.

Michael switched on the light and they shot him, the tall one first and then the other, the impact hurling Michael back against the headboard, skewing him round until his face finished somehow pressed up against the wall.

Moving closer, the shorter of the two wrenched the wire from the socket and the room went dark. Too late to prevent Eileen from seeing what she had seen: the taller man bareheaded, more than bare, shaven, bald, a child's mask, Mickey Mouse, covering the centre of his face; his companion had a woollen hat pulled low, a red scarf wrapped high around his neck and jaw. Some of Michael's blood ran, slow and warm, between Eileen's arm and her breast. The rest was pooling between his legs, spreading dark across the sheets. The sound she hadn't recognised was her own choked sobbing, caught like a hairball in her throat. She knew they would kill her or rape her or both.

'You want it?' the shorter one said, gesturing towards the bed.

The tall one made a sound like someone about to throw up and the shorter one laughed.

Eileen closed her eyes and when she opened them again they had gone.

Welcoming the rare chance of an early night, Lynn Kellogg had been in bed for a good hour by the time Resnick returned home. Through several layers of sleep she registered the Saab slowing into the drive outside, the front door closing firmly in its frame, feet slow but heavy on the stairs; sounds from the bathroom and then his weight on the mattress as he lowered himself down.

More than two years now and she still sometimes felt it strange, this man beside her in her bed. His bed, to be more precise.

'God, Charlie,' she said, shifting her legs. 'Your feet are like blocks of ice. And you stink of beer.' His mumbled apology seemed to merge with his first snore. His feet might be cold, but the rest of him seemed to radiate warmth. Lynn moved close against him and within not so many minutes she was asleep again herself.

Short of four, the phone woke them both.

'Yours or mine?' Resnick said, pushing back the covers.

'Mine.'

She was already on her feet, starting to pull on clothes.

'Shooting,' she said, when she'd put the phone back down. 'Tattershall Drive.'

'You want me to come?'

Lynn shook her head. 'No need. Go back to sleep.'

When they'd started living together, Lynn had transferred from Resnick's squad into Major Crime; less messy that way. Her coat, a hooded black anorak, windproof and waterproof, was on a hook in the hall. Despite the hour, it was surprisingly light outside, not so far off a full moon.

The body had not yet been moved. Scene of Crime were taking photographs, measuring, assiduously taking samples from the floor. The pathologist was still on his way. It didn't need an expert, Lynn thought, to see how he'd died.

Anil Khan stood beside her in the doorway. He had been the first officer from the Major Crime unit to arrive.

'Two of them, so she says.' His voice was light, barely accented.

'She?'

'Wife, mistress, whatever. She's downstairs.'

Lynn nodded. When she had been promoted, three months before, detective sergeant to detective inspector, Khan had slipped easily into her shoes.

'Any idea how they got in?'

'Bedroom window, by the look of things. Out through the front door.'

Lynn glanced across the room. 'Flew in then, like Peter Pan?'

Khan smiled. 'Ladder marks on the sill.'

Eileen was sitting in a leather armchair, quilt round her shoulders, no trace of colour in her face. Someone had made her a cup of tea and it sat on a lacquered table, untouched. The room itself was large and unlived in, heavy dark furniture, dark paintings in ornamental frames; wherever they'd spent their time, Lynn thought, it wasn't here.

She lifted a high-backed wooden chair and carried it across the room.

Through the partly open door she saw Khan escorting the pathologist towards the stairs. She set the chair down at an angle, close to Eileen, and introduced herself, name and rank. Eileen continued to stare into space, barely registering that she was there.

'Can you tell me what happened?' Lynn said.

No reply.

'I need you to tell me what happened,' Lynn said. For a moment, she touched Eileen's hand.

'I already did. I told the Paki.'

'Tell me. In your own time.'

Eileen looked at her then. 'They killed him. What more d'you want to know?'

'Everything,' Lynn said. 'Everything.'

His name was Michael Sandler: Mikhail Sharminov. He had come to England from Russia fifteen years before. Born in Tbilisi, Georgia, to Russo-Armenian parents, as a young man he had quickly decided a life devoted to the production of citrus fruit and tung oil was not for him. He went, as a student, to Moscow, and by the time he was thirty he had a thriving business importing bootlegged rock music through East Germany into Russia, everything from the Beatles to Janis Joplin. Soon, there were video tapes, bootlegged also: *Apocalypse Now, The Godfather, ET*. By the standards of the Russian black economy, Mikhail was on his way to being rich. But then, by 1989 the Berlin Wall was crumbling and, in its wake, the Union of Soviet Socialist Republics was falling apart. Georgia, where his ageing parents still lived, was on the verge of civil war. Free trade loomed. Go or stay? Mikhail became Michael.

In Britain he used his capital to build up a chain of

provincial video stores, most of whose profits came from pirated DVDs; some of his previous contacts in East Berlin were now in Taiwan, in Tirana, in Hong Kong. Truly, a global economy. Michael Sandler, fifty-eight years old. The owner outright of property to the value of two million-five, together with the leases of more than a dozen stores; three bank accounts, one offshore; a collection of paintings, including a small Kandinsky worth an estimated eight hundred and fifty thousand pounds; three cars, a Lexus and two BMWs; four .38 bullets, fired from close range, two high in the chest, one to the temple, one that had torn through his throat.

Most of this information Lynn Kellogg amassed over the following days and weeks, piecing together local evidence with what could be gleaned from national records and H.M. Customs and Excise. And long before that, before the end of that first conversation, she realised she had seen Eileen before.

'Charlie,' she said, phoning him at home. 'I think you'd better get over here after all.' The first time Resnick had set eyes on Eileen, she'd been sitting in a basement wine bar, smoking a cigarette and drinking Bacardi and Coke, her hair redder then and falling loose around her shoulders. The harshness of her make-up, in that attenuated light, had been softened; her silver-grey top, like pale filigree, shimmered a little with each breath she took. She knew he was staring at her and thought little of it: it was what people did. Men, mostly. It was what, until she'd taken up with Terry Cooke, had paid her way in the world.

The sandwich Resnick had ordered arrived and when he bit into it mayonnaise smeared across the palm of his hand; through the bar stereo Parker was stripping the sentiment from 'Don't Blame Me' – New York City, 1947, the closing bars of Miles' muted trumpet aside, it's Bird's alto all the way, acrid and languorous, and when it's over there's nothing left to do or say.

'You bastard!' Eileen had yelled later. 'You fucking bastard! Making out you're so fucking sympathetic and understanding and all the while you're screwing me just as much as those bastards who think for fifty quid they can bend me over some car park wall and fuck me up the arse.'

A nice turn of phrase, Eileen, and Resnick, while he might have resisted the graphic nature of her metaphor, would have had to admit she was right.

He had wanted to apply pressure to Terry Cooke and his burgeoning empire of low-grade robbers and villains, and in Eileen, in what he had misread as her weakness, he thought he had seen the means.

'Leave him,' he'd said. 'Give us something we can make stick. Circumstances like this, you've got to look out for yourself. No one would blame you for that.'

In the end it had been Terry who had weakened and whether it had been his fear of getting caught and being locked away that had made him pull the trigger, or his fear of losing Eileen, Resnick would never know. After the funeral, amidst the fall-out and recriminations, she had slipped from sight and it was some time before he saw her again, close to desperate and frightened, so frightened that he had offered her safe haven in that same big sprawling house where he now lived with Lynn, and there, in the long sparse hours between sleeping and waking, she had slid into his bed and fallen fast asleep, one of her legs across his and her head so light against his chest it could almost have been a dream.

Though his history of relationships was neither extensive nor particularly successful, and though he prized honesty above most other things, he knew enough never to have mentioned this incident to Lynn, innocent as he would vainly have tried to make it seem.

He stood now in the doorway, a bulky man with a shape-less suit and sagging eyes, and waited until, aware of his presence, she turned her head.

'Hello, Eileen.'

The sight of him brought tears to her eyes. 'Christ, Charlie. First Terry and now this. Getting to be too much of a fucking habit, if you ask me.' She held out a hand and he took it, and then she pressed her head against the rough weave of his coat, the too soft flesh beneath, and cried.

After several moments, Resnick rested his other hand against her shoulder, close to the nape of her neck, and that's how they were some minutes later when Lynn looked into the room through the open door, then looked away.

'What did she have to say for herself?' Lynn asked later. They were high on The Ropewalk, the light breaking through the sky, bits and pieces of the city waking south and west below them.

'No more, I dare say, than she told you,' Resnick said.

'Don't tell me all that compassion went for nothing.'

Resnick bridled. 'She'd just seen her bloke shot dead alongside her, what was I supposed to do?'

Lynn gave a small shake of the head. 'It's okay, Charlie. Just teasing.'

'I'm glad to hear it.'

'Though I do wonder if you had to look as if you were enjoying it quite as much.'

At the end of the street they stopped. Canning Circus police station, where Resnick was based, was only a few minutes away.

'What do you think?' Lynn asked. 'A paid hit?'

'I doubt it was a couple of local tearaways out to make a name for themselves. Whoever this was, they'll be well up the motorway by now. Up or down.'

'Someone he'd crossed.'

'Likely.'

'Business, then.'

'Whatever that is.'

Lynn breathed in deeply, drawing the air down into her lungs. 'I'd best get started.'

'Okay.'

'See you tonight.'

'Yes.'

She stood for a moment, watching him walk away. Her imagination, or was he slower than he used to be? Turning, she retraced her steps to where she'd parked her car.

Much of the next few days Lynn spent accessing and exchanging information on the computer and speaking on the telephone, building up, as systematically as she could, a picture of Mikhail Sharminov's activities, while forensic staff analysed the evidence provided by Scene of Crime.

At the start of the following week, Lynn, armed with a bulging briefcase and a new Next suit, went to a meeting at the headquarters of the Specialist Crime Directorate in London; also present were officers from the National Criminal Intelligence Service and the National Crime Squad, as well as personnel from H.M. Customs and Excise, and observers from the Interpol team that was carrying out a long-term investigation into the Russian mafia.

By the time the meeting came to a halt, some six hours and several coffee breaks later, Lynn's head was throbbing with unfamiliar names and all-too familiar motivations. Sharminov, it seemed, had been seen as an outsider within the Soviet diaspora; as far as possible he had held himself apart, relying instead on his contacts in the Far East. But with the increased capability for downloading not only CDs but now DVDs via the Internet, the logistics of his chosen field were changing, markets were shifting and becoming more specialised. There was a burgeoning trade in hard-core pornography which certain of Sharminov's former compatriots were keen to further through the networks he'd established. For a price. It wasn't clear whether he had resisted on moral grounds or because the price wasn't right.

Eileen was questioned at length about Sharminov's business partners and shown numerous photographs, the faces in which, for the most part, she failed to recognise. One man, middle-aged, with dark close-cropped hair and eyes too close together, had been to the house on several occasions, hurried conversations behind closed doors; another, silver-haired and leonine, she remembered seeing once, albeit briefly, in the rear seat of a limousine. There were others, a few, of whom she was less certain.

'Did he seem worried lately?' they asked her. 'Concerned about business?'

'No,' she said. 'Not especially.'

Perhaps he should have been. The silver-haired man was Alexei Popov, whose organisation encompassed drugs and pornography and human trafficking in a network that stretched from the Bosphorus and the Adriatic to the English Channel, and had particularly strong links with the Turkish and Italian mafia. Tony Christanidi was his go-between and sometime enforcer, the kind of middle-management executive who never left home without first checking that his two-shot .22 Derringer was snug alongside his mobile phone.

The line back through Christanidi to Popov was suspected of being behind three recent fatal shootings, one in Manchester, one in Marseilles, the other in Tirana.

'Would they carry out these shootings themselves?' Lynn had asked.

'Not usually. Sometimes they'll make a deal with the Turks or the Sicilians. You do one for me, I'll do one for you. Other times, they'll simply contract it out. Usually overseas. Someone flies in, picks up the weapons locally, junks them straight after, twelve hours later they're back on the plane.'

'So they wouldn't necessarily be English?'

'Not at all.'

'The two men who shot Sharminov, the only witness we have swears they were English.'

'This is the girlfriend?'

'Eileen. Yes.'

'I don't understand.'

'What?'

'Why they didn't kill her too.'

'You don't think she could have been involved?'

'In setting him up? I suppose it's possible.'

They questioned Eileen again, pushed her hard until her confidence was in shreds and her voice was gone.

'I don't think she knows anything,' the National Crime Squad officer said after almost four hours of interrogation. 'She was just lucky, that's all.'

She wasn't the only one. Good luck and bad. In the early hours of the morning, almost two weeks and two days after Mikhail Sharminov was murdered, there was a shooting in the city. At around two in the morning, there was an altercation at the roundabout linking Canal Street with London Road, a Range Rover cutting across a BMW and causing the driver to brake hard. After a lot of gesturing and angry shouting, the Range Rover drove off at speed, the other vehicle following. At the lights midway along Queen's Drive, where it runs beside the Trent, the BMW came alongside and the man in the passenger seat leaned out and shot the driver of the Range Rover five times.

The driver was currently in a critical condition in hospital, hanging on. Forensics suggested that the shots had been fired from one of the same weapons that had been used to kill Mikhail Sharminov, a snub-nosed .38 Smith and Wesson.

'It could mean whoever shot Sharminov was recruited locally after all,' Lynn said. 'Didn't see any need to leave town.'

They were in the kitchen of the house in Mapperley, Saturday afternoon: Lynn ironing, a glass of white wine close at hand; Resnick putting together a salad with half an ear cocked towards the radio, the soccer commentary on Five Live.

'Well, he has now,' Resnick said, wondering why the bottle of walnut oil was always right at the back of the cupboard when you needed it. Neither the driver nor the passenger of the BMW had so far been traced.

'You think it's possible?' Lynn said.

Resnick shook a few drops of the oil over rocket and romaine and reached for the pepper. 'I think you're on safer ground following the gun.' He broke off a piece of lettuce to taste, scowled, and began ferreting for the Tabasco.

'Don't make it too hot, Charlie. You always do.'

'Assume they've flown in. Birmingham, Leeds-Bradford, East Midlands. There's a meeting with whoever's supplying the weapons, prearranged. After the job, either they're dumped or, more likely, handed back.'

'Recycled.'

'I could still tell you which pub to go to if you wanted a converted replica. A hundred in tens handed over in the Gents. But this is a different league.'

'Bernard Vitori,' Lynn said. 'He's the best bet. Eddie Chambers, possibly. One or two others. We'll start with Vitori first thing.'

'Sunday morning?' Resnick said. 'He won't like that.'

'Disturbing his day of rest?'

'Takes his mother to church. Strelley Road Baptists.

Regular as clockwork.' Resnick ran a finger round the inside of the salad bowl. 'Here. Taste this. Tell me what you think.'

They followed Vitori and his mum to church, thirty officers, some armed, keeping the building tightly surrounded, mingling inside. The preacher was delighted by the increase in his congregation. Sixty or so minutes of energetic testifying later, Vitori reluctantly unlocked the boot of his car. Snug inside were a 9mm Glock 17 and a Chinese-made A15 semi-automatic rifle. Vitori had been taking them to a potential customer after the service. Faced with the possibility of eight to ten inside, he cut a deal. Contact with the Russians had been by mobile phone, using numbers which were now untraceable, names which were clearly fake. Vitori had met two men in the Little Chef on the A60, north of Arnold. Leased them two clean revolvers for twenty-four hours, seven hundred the pair. Three days later, he'd sold one of the guns to a known drug dealer for five hundred more.

No matter how many times officers from Interpol and NICS showed him photographs of potential hit men, Vitori claimed to recognise none. He was not only happy to name the dealer, furnishing an address into the bargain, he gave them a likely identity for the driver of the car. Remanded in custody, special pleading would get him a five year sentence at most, of which he'd serve less than three.

'Bloody Russians, Charlie,' Peter Waites said, sitting opposite Resnick in their usual pub. 'When I was a kid we were always waiting for them to blow us up. Now they're over here like fucking royalty.'

Sensing a rant coming, Resnick nodded noncommittally and supped his beer.

'That bloke owns Chelsea football club. Abramovich? He's not the only one, you know. This Boris, for instance – what's his name? – Berezovsky. One of the richest people in the fucking country. More money than the fucking Queen.'

Resnick sensed it was not the time to remind Waites that as a dedicated republican, he thought Buckingham Palace should be turned into council housing and Her Majesty forced to live out her remaining years on her old age pension.

'You know how many Russians there are in this country, Charlie? According to the last census?'

Resnick shook his head. Waites had been spending too much time in Bolsover library, trawling the Internet for free. 'I give up, Peter,' he said. 'Tell me.'

'Forty thousand, near as damn it. And they're not humping bricks for a few quid an hour on building sites or picking cockles in Morecambe fucking Bay. Living in bloody luxury, that's what they're doing.' Leaning forward, Waites jabbed a finger urgently towards Resnick's face. 'Every third property in London sold to a foreign citizen last year went to a bloody Russian. Every fifteenth property sold for over half a million the same.' He shook his head. 'This country, Charlie. Last ten, twenty years, it's turned upside fucking down.' He wiped his mouth with the back of his hand.

'Another?' Resnick said, pointing to Waites' empty glass.

'Go on. Why not?'

For a good ten minutes neither man spoke. Noise and smoke spiralled around them. Laughter but not too much of that. The empty trill of slot machines from the far side of the bar.

'This soccer thing, Charlie,' Waites said eventually. 'Yanks buying into Manchester United and now there's this President of Thailand or whatever, wants forty per cent of Liverpool so's he can flog Steven Gerrard shirts all over South-East Asia. It's not football any more, Charlie, it's all fucking business. Global fuckin' economy.' He drank deep and drained his glass. 'It's the global fucking economy as has thrown me and hundreds like me onto the fucking scrap heap, that's what it's done.' Waites sighed and shook his head. 'Sorry, Charlie. You ought never to have let me get started.'

'Stopping you'd take me and seven others.'

'Happen so.'

At the door Waites stopped to light a cigarette. 'You know what really grates with me, Charlie? It used to be a working class game, football. Now they've took that from us as well.'

'Some places,' Resnick said, 'it still is.'

'Come on, Charlie. What's happening, you don't think it's right no more'n I do.'

'Maybe not. Though I wouldn't mind some oil billionaire from Belarus taking a fancy to Notts County for a spell. Buy 'em a halfway decent striker, someone with a bit of nous for midfield.'

Waites laughed. 'Now who's whistling in the dark?'

For several months Customs and Excise and others did their best to unravel Sharminov's financial affairs; his stock was seized, his shops closed down. A further six months down the line, Alexei Popov would buy them through a twice-removed subsidiary and begin trading in DVDs for what was euphemistically called the adult market. He also bought a flat in Knightsbridge for a cool five million, close to the one owned by Roman Abramovich, though there was no indication the two men knew one another. Abramovich's Chelsea continued to prosper; no oil-fed angel came to Notts County's rescue as they struggled against relegation.

Lynn began to wonder if a sideways move into the National Crime Squad might help to refocus her career.

Resnick saw Eileen one more time. Although most of the money belonging to the man she knew as Michael Sandler had been confiscated, she had inherited enough for new clothes and an expensive makeover, new suitcases which were waiting in the taxi parked outside.

'I thought I'd travel, Charlie. See the world. Switzerland, maybe. Fly round some mountains.' Her smile was near to perfect. 'You know the only place I've been abroad? If you don't count the Isle of Man. Alicante. Apart from the heat, it wasn't like being abroad at all. Even the announcements in the supermarket were in English.'

'Enjoy it,' Resnick said. 'Have a good time.'

Eileen laughed. 'Come with me, why don't you? Chuck it all in. About time you retired.'

'Thanks a lot.'

For a moment her face went serious. 'You think we could ever have got together, Charlie?'

'In another life, maybe.'

'Which life is that?'

Resnick smiled. 'The one where I'm ten years younger and half a stone lighter; not already living with somebody else.'

'And not a policeman?'

'Maybe that too.'

Craning upwards, she kissed him quickly on the lips. 'You're a good man, Charlie, and don't let anyone tell you otherwise.'

Long after she had gone, he could feel the pressure of her mouth on his and smell the scent of her skin beneath the new perfume.

For K.C. Constantine, with gratitude and admiration, in particular for his marvellous novel, Blood Mud, *from which the salad finger episode was borrowed, with permission.*

'GOING ANYWHERE NICE?'

(A Mr Grubshaw and Woody Story)

Lindsey Davis

'Goin' anywhere nice for your 'oliday?'

Immediately, Renzo was summoned by his mobile phone. A computerised trill from *La Forza del Destino* left Mr Grubshaw thwarted. Renzo stepped outside to lean his paunch against the doorframe and engage in impenetrable Sardinian business chat.

According to Renzo, he was the best barber in Deptford. Certainly Mr Grubshaw went into the shop feeling untidy and came out different – though passers-by then peered at him as if he resembled a conman on *Crimewatch* who was being sought by three police forces for emptying old ladies' bank accounts.

Renzo's shop was owned by Halycon Properties, a front for two Lebanese brothers with big ideas and dodgy spelling. They had run a VAT racket on mobile phones until Customs and Excise tightened up the rules; now they were planning to rent out student bedsits. Until they put in place the finance for installing faulty gas water-heaters, Renzo hung on, alongside Cursing Khaleed, whose tiny café was filled with cigarette smoke and thin men of Balkan appearance who did nothing all day.

'Grubby' Grubshaw was sole proprietor of the XYZ Detective Agency, though Renzo, who was curiously uninterested in his customers, had never discovered this. The private eye had wandered into the barber's once when the Department of Social Services, for whom he did occasional fraud enquiries, asked him to watch a Chinese man who seemed to be claiming for a non-existent wife. Mrs Cheung's body then washed up on the bank of the Thames, so the DSS lost interest because she was perfectly entitled to benefits, had Mr Cheung not murdered her. The police hijacked Mr Grubshaw's casenotes, complimenting him on their neatness and detail (he had written them up hastily, with his niece's help, the night before). Then Cheung fled the country, so even the police lost interest. At least Grubby had acquired a barber.

Renzo was cheap. He was gloomy and introspective, but when he bothered he could cut hair well. He made a tasteless joke of 'Don' worry, I no cut your throat!' to anyone who risked a wet shave – but Mr Grubshaw had seen too many films about the Chicago Mob to relax in a chair while lathered up. He only ever braved a trim. Normally, by the time Renzo asked if he had any holiday plans and he replied not really, it was all over. Today, Grubby experienced slight disappointment; the mobile phonecall prevented him announcing that for once he was taking his niece to the Bay of Naples. He had hoped a Mediterranean destination would impress Renzo.

'Business colleagues; big people,' the barber boasted, shoving away the phone and clicking his scissors alarmingly. He seemed put out by the call. He muttered in his home dialect, then flashed a brazen grin. 'Big people who need Renzo! Very special job . . .'

That sounded far too much like Sweeney Todd. Mr Grubshaw avoided discussing his holiday and fled.

Back at his office, his niece was busy at his computer. The XYZ Detective Agency was another Halycon Properties rental, two upstairs rooms with rotten floors, over a bank-rupt software firm. It made an unsuitable haven for a twelve-year-old girl, but both her parents worked, so Mr Grubshaw took her in after school. Perdita ('call me Tracey') kept his records in order for him.

'I've booked everything online with Dad's credit card,' she sniggered. It made a change from her buying CDs with Mr Grubshaw's own card. A pale thing with bunches in scrunchies, whose wardrobe was dominated by pink leggings and big black shoes, she vacuumed relatives' PIN numbers from their minds by osmosis. 'He's sending us Business Class.'

'Oh! . . . Does Clive know you use his card?'

'He will!'

Mr Grubshaw's youngest brother, a 'respectable' City broker, had caused the Naples trip. Finding his niece in tears a week earlier, Mr Grubshaw discovered that Clive had left home, to be with his young assistant. 'Fiona – ugh! She's having a baby.' Something worse had caused the tears: 'Dad forgot to pay for my school trip.' Grubby stepped in to take Tracey and her mother Jean to see the archaeological sites.

They were not the only people heading towards Vesuvius: as they entered the airport boarding lounge, Mr Grubshaw was convinced he spotted Renzo, though the barber had his head in a phone booth. Grubby said nothing, a professional habit, and since Business Class was boarded last there was no awkward eye contact.

During the flight, Tracey kept her CD player welded to both ears, listening to Mortal Dread and the Troubled Minds, so her uncle could give her mother legal advice. Clive had money, but allocating any to Tracey's upkeep might become tricky; there were signs that Fiona had spent her time as a finance assistant learning how to ensure *her* life would be a soft one.

'Constant "late business meetings", then he claims *I* lost interest!' ranted Jean, who was still adapting to her loss of status as part of a yuppie couple. They had bought a four-storey Georgian house in Greenwich before the Docklands Light Railway was brought across the river, causing a knee-jerk in prices. 'We were planning to upgrade to a five-storey, cashing in. Now he says I can buy him out – how, exactly, on teaching Comparative Literature four days a week? They maintain they are slumming in a flat – but it's a flat with Philippe Starck washbasins! All I ever got was Villeroy and Boch, installed by plumbers who took eight months – and we never did get the right loo handle . . .' After years of despising Grubby for his informal lifestyle, she now suspected she had married the wrong brother; it made for an intriguing family atmosphere. 'I've been blind. Do you think there were others?'

'There may have been, Jean.'

'I suppose it's the oldest deceit.'

'It's been known,' Grubby agreed.

'I could kill him!'

'That's been done,' said Grubby sadly.

'Would a private detective suggest a contract killer?'

'My code requires me to advise against it, Jean.'

'I don't even need you to find evidence; he bloody told me everything himself . . . Well, I hope you haven't brought that damned matchbox!' Jean was denouncing the container where Grubby kept a woodlouse who allegedly helped solve cases. When he merely looked innocent, she exploded, 'Oh no! What if we're searched by Customs?'

'Woody has a pet passport,' grinned Tracey, holding an earplug aside.

The pilot was mumbling on the muffly intercom. 'Alter your watches,' deciphered Mr Grubshaw alertly, winding his on an hour. 'Get back to Mort, Trace, while I instruct your mother on how to fleece your father.'

They stayed at a shoreline hotel by the Castel d'Ovo, an old fortress with a harbourful of boats nodding their masts at the foot of the keep. They had splendid views across the bay, out to Capri, which was visible on clear nights as a scatter of pale lights. From their balconies, they could turn towards Mount Vesuvius and wonder whether that was a faint trace of smoke threading upwards from the crater . . .

Before dinner, Mr Grubshaw lay on one of the twin beds in his room, reading a free newspaper from the plane. Having assured Jean that all the Vespa-riding bag-snatchers had been cleared out of Naples in Millennium Year, he had concealed from her an article discussing problems with Mafia drug-sellers. There was uproar on some impoverished estates because the local Camorra was trying to impose a new business plan on pushers.

'Must have been on a management course!' Grubby glanced across to the second bed, where a matchbox reposed on the pillow just where chambermaids deposit a chocolate to remind guests to leave a tip. 'Reminds me of that brochure I chucked in the bin: *Participants will learn how to:*

- **Formulate** a stratetic market plan
- **Organise** activities to bring in new business
- **Develop** a marketing culture in their organisation
- **Motivate** colleagues to achieve agreed commitments

Pretty straightforward, Woody. Some dealer annoys you with his feeble marketing culture, you shoot dead his young girl-friend.' He read on. 'Guns in the street – mainly at weekends. The Camorra must all hold down nice jobs . . . No-go tower blocks, where dealers have installed security cameras to show the police arriving; then they've put metal gates on stair-wells to hold the officers up . . . Just like home, Woody. Let's hope the Deptford pushers don't take holidays to get ideas.'

Woody said nothing, being a reticent character.

The family set out on foot for dinner. Lights across the causeway to the fortress attracted them, but they decided to head further afield, turning past a row of elegant old hotels. Outside the grandest a limousine pulled up. A chauffeur in a classic blue blazer escorted an elderly couple across the pavement towards a flunkey in a maroon tailcoat. The couple looked like local VIPs on some regular night out at a hotel restaurant.

Tracey marched up, a self-assured child. The woman tolerantly paused to let her pass. Jean smiled their thanks and scuttled out of the way. Lagging in the rear, Mr Grubshaw noticed that Signor looked annoyed at being kept waiting. The man had a quiet manner, yet expected to be given precedence, even by strangers. His chauffeur's attitude was tellingly different.

'The Mayor of Naples?' wondered Jean.

'Gangland racketeer,' her daughter suggested.

'Successful accountant and wife,' murmured Grubby. 'Meeting friends for a bridge party.'

'I don't *think* so!' scoffed Tracey.

Replete after their Business Class dinner earlier, the family settled for pizzas. As they tucked in, Tracey explained the terms on which this holiday was to be conducted: the group from her school were staying at a cheaper hotel along the bay and would pick her up every morning as their coach passed by. Tracey did not want to be embarrassed at archaeological sites by the presence of relatives, so Jean and Grubby had to visit other locations. Nobody wanted Trouble, so this was agreed.

Accordingly, when the schoolgirls visited Pompeii, Jean

and Grubby went to Herculaneum using the Circumvesuvio railway. While the school party were at Herculaneum, the others crossed by ferry to Capri. The day the girls saw Poppaea's Villa at Oplontis, Jean and Grubby managed a morning in Naples Museum; they went up there by taxi, then afterwards walked back down a long road towards their hotel, window-shopping. They made one quick foray uphill into narrower alleys, but did not linger. Mr Grubshaw was remembering the newspaper article's description of a drug-dealer being shot in a salami shop, among hams and prosciutto salesmen. Dead meat.

'That's enough backstreet Neapolitan atmosphere! Let's find an ice-cream.'

Returning to the main road, they came across an enormous glass-roofed gallery, its cross-shaped interior lined with banks, cafés, jewellers and incongruous electrical shops. Jean's guide-book identified the Galleria Umberto I. While she admired the grey and pale gold marble floor of one gracious arcade, Mr Grubshaw noticed through the farthermost exit a faded building across the street. Tall rectangular windows were flanked by dark green louvred shutters. Outside one window, two men talked on a balcony, perhaps avoiding eavesdroppers. He realised that there, discreetly placed above a Solarium, was a business close to his heart: an International Detective Agency.

He took a closer look. A man, much like himself, though with a smarter jacket, emerged at street level, hands in pockets. He sauntered into the Galleria. It seemed the wrong place for a detective to spend his lunch break – at least until he stationed himself outside an electrical shop, studying cut-price vacuum cleaners.

Jean had found a pavement table for a cappuccino. She whispered excitedly, 'There's that racketeer from the other evening!'

'Merely a toasted-pannini mogul.' Grubby stuck to his theory that the man was mundane.

'The couple looked too respectable to *be* respectable. I should know. Think of Clive! The bastard is smooching his trophy mistress – believe me.'

Mr Grubshaw mildly followed her gaze. The man they had seen entering the hotel restaurant on their first night was indeed enjoying an expresso with a much-younger woman, though he was not bothering to smooch her. They knew each other *far* better than that. This was their regular lunchtime rendezvous; Grubby conceded that no Italian boss would routinely take his secretary to lunch.

She wore a wide-shouldered tan leather coat loosely over her shoulders, its collar brushed by expensively streaked blonde hair. She had a confident personality and was speaking, not angrily but at length. A chunky gold bracelet pulled the cuff of her cashmere sweater as she gesticulated passionately. Grubby remarked that she looked like a woman who did most things passionately and Jean joked, 'Except the dusting!'

As a bachelor in a solo business, Mr Grubshaw had chosen life on his own terms. To see another male under such pressure made him queasy.

The man remained calm, replying only briefly. Eventually reassured, his companion left half the coffee that had been bought for her, air-kissed her lover, then left. She walked briskly, calling greetings to a female friend outside a boutique. She looked open about her meeting and the man, too, was powerful enough not to be furtive. Well, not unless his wife strolled through the Galleria. She was unlikely to confront him; that couple had plenty of secrets, Grubby thought, and they would keep their arguments private.

The private detective now acted the tourist, and took photographs. He had already snapped the lovers at their café, especially when they kissed farewell. He took a long view of the woman disappearing down the arcade, then sauntered nonchalantly to gaze at a display of slightly trashy art.

The businessman stayed at the café. Grubby encouraged Jean to indulge in a pastry.

'The price is a rip-off.'

'Relax. We're on holiday.'

'You sound like your brother sometimes.'

'Good old Clive!'

Grubby was quietly watching his colleague, who was now chatting to an ice-cream vendor. The businessman grew bored, checked his watch with the waiter, and stood up. He dropped a large euro note on the table, though no bill had been presented.

The detective hung around.

Jean wanted to move, but Grubby had seen a familiar paunchy figure. Renzo, his barber, wandered through an arcade, was distracted by a camera shop, stared three times at the café the businessman had vacated, then chose that one for a snack. Casually, one-handed as he licked an ice-cream, the private eye photographed him.

Renzo drank two expressos and demolished a sandwich with the savagery he used on Cursing Khaleed's vegetarian kebabs back in Deptford. Apparently waiting for someone, he glanced repeatedly at his watch, tried to call someone on his mobile, failed, paid up, and mooched off. The detective then went for a word with the waiter, who indicated his own wristwatch; they laughed.

'Alter your watches . . . Renzo's in the wrong time zone, Jean!'

Banned by Tracey from all archaeological sites that day, Jean and Grubby whiled away the afternoon locally. The

Piazza del Plebiscito was an elliptical colonnaded public space, with a church modelled on the Pantheon in Rome and a resident group of lazy town dogs; dramatically sited with views of the bay, they found the Palazzo Reale. Since it was free, they took a relaxed circuit through its astonishingly restored rooms. It had all the glamour of Versailles without the crowds. They finally emerged, sated with enormous Sèvres urns and Gobelin tapestries. Desperate to rest their legs, they headed for Gambrinus, Naples' oldest corner café where they could pretend to be genteel amid faded paintings of roses, as Oscar Wilde had done. There were tables outside, but they chose the interior, the better to torment themselves with the sight of delectable chocolate cakes.

'Well, at least Signora gets out!' Jean's angry mutter alerted Mr Grubshaw to three mature ladies with smart carrier bags. 'Do you think she knows he's two-timing her?'

'Yes; here comes the chauffeur with the prints of Signor and his trophy friend.'

'Signora looks such a nice woman.'

'Mafia mommas have a reputation. I wouldn't cross her.'

'I wonder if they have children?'

'Probably.' But how many were dead in the drug wars?

'He must have strayed before,' snarled Jean, with fellow-feeling, as the elderly woman took the stiff envelope her driver had brought and opened it calmly. She half pulled the photos out, glancing at them as if what she found was only what she expected. One of her friends was stirring her cup; the other gathered herself for a trip to the Ladies. They had hardly acknowledged the chauffeur's arrival, but Grubby thought they both knew what he had brought. 'Plenty of times!' Jean was still harping on.

Grubby remembered the businessman's girlfriend, with

her strong walk and her air of having life before her. 'This particular young lady wants it all,' he decided.

'Oh, a *Fiona*!' Jean went into a bitter reverie. 'She wasn't as young as she'd like men to think.'

'So she's a worse threat.'

Viewing the evidence, Signora looked as though she wasn't finished yet. Kept separate from her husband's work, no doubt, she probably knew a lot about it even so. In their early years together she would have helped his struggle to establish himself. Grubby sniggered. 'If *Signora* decides she wants it all too, do you think that includes the chauffeur?'

Jean considered, though not for long. 'He's nothing special.'

The other two mature ladies chatted to the waiting driver, informally; they knew him of old. Signora tapped the photo set back into its envelope, which she dropped into her large designer bag. She dismissed the chauffeur with a nod. All three ladies appeared to continue their previous conversation.

'Catholics,' whispered Jean. 'No divorce.'

'I expect the priest will give him a good talking to.' That would not have deterred Clive, when tackled by a determined finance assistant who wanted his baby and his bonds.

'No divorce – but plenty of retribution, Grubby!'

The husband might anticipate the retribution and want to deflect it. Grubby felt chilled.

He considered warning the private detectives that their bourgeois female client, now eating coffee-iced torte, could be the subject of Renzo's 'special job'. But if she were his client, he would frostily refuse any discussion with an outsider. Maybe it was all right. The detective had photographed Renzo; that was significant. If Signor had plans, Signora was ahead of him.

Another chill caused Grubby to call time and return to the hotel so they were ready to greet Tracey when the coach brought her back.

'Well, that was real interior design! It was like, well, *themed*.' Tracey had enjoyed Poppaea's Villa, a two-thousand-year-old masterpiece of décor. 'There were hundreds of rooms and some had, like, spooky masks painted, but the best bit was the outdoor swimming pool. You could hold a *wicked* barbecue—'

'I expect they did,' said Grubby drily.

'What has been your favourite site, Perdita?' The teacher in Jean relied on constant evaluation. (How sad, therefore, that she had spent so little time evaluating Clive . . .)

'Oh Mum. If you had to call me after somebody in Shakespeare, I wish you'd chosen someone with some style.'

'Goneril?' suggested Jean waspishly, immediately regretting it.

'Great!' Tracey was now Goneril. 'The brothel at Pompeii was quite good.' Jean and Grubby exchanged a surreptitious glance. They had not even found the brothel, let alone negotiated an entry price with its legendary smarmy keyholder. 'Capri was *gross*; you could really imagine terrible old Tiberius hurling his enemies off the crag—' Jean nodded, newly eager to hear of men being cast to their deaths unpleasantly. 'The best was Vesuvius and the hot springs at the Phlegraian Fields. A vulcanologist explained how Naples is doomed. Every year that Vesuvius fails to erupt now, means a bigger explosion when it next blows its top. Millions of people are going to be trapped . . .'

Mr Grubshaw wondered if people who lived in the shadow of a recognised future disaster might be more prone to violence. He discarded the theory. The only difference between Naples and Deptford was that the villains in Deptford were multi-cultural, while the rival clans in Naples came from one gene pool. Presumably it went all the way back to the peasants who were buried in pumice or molten mud in Pliny's day.

That made him think. Renzo would be a foreigner here. Someone commissioning a special job, a job that broke even the rules of this tight-knit community – deleting a *wife and mother*, say, the matriarch of a clan – might well bring in an outside agent. A Sardinian could have the expertise without the local sensitivity. He could settle a domestic issue without causing decades of Neapolitan blood-feud, and afterwards he could fly off back where he came from.

But Renzo, with his vacant manner and so inefficient he had failed to set his watch to local time, was a bad choice. He might share a criminal background and very dangerous skills, but his stubble darkened the wrong-shaped chin. His dialect probably sounded as thick here as it did in Deptford. Word of his presence would whiz around. The women with neatly pressed tweed jackets and straight skirts who toyed with *limoncelli* in smart cafés possessed just as effective networks as their men. And they probably had their own agents of destruction too.

Whether Signor realised he was rumbled would depend on him. The mouthy young woman in the leather coat must be doing her best to undermine Signora's importance in his eyes. An arrogant man, easily flattered by a feisty mistress, might forget that, although Signora had staff at home these days and no longer toiled over *osso bucco* on a hot stove, she still knew the recipe.

That evening Mr Grubshaw rationalised his own position. 'Woody, I could report my suspicions to the police and be laughed at. I could drop a wink at the detective agency and be seen off as a batty menace. I've no proof of anything, and if challenged, Renzo will claim he's on holiday, just like me.'

The woodlouse said nothing, but did it sympathetically. To give him an airing, Grubby carried the matchbox out into the balcony. Its concrete was unwelcoming to a creature who lived on rotten wood in damp places, but together the two friends gazed at the ocean. A perfect moon had risen above the Castel d'Ovo. Lights from a cruise ship slowly moved out towards Capri in the darkness. To the right of the causeway, a small boat could just be discerned where lethargic fishermen tended lobsterpots every morning in tethered ranks between the shore and the hydrofoil routes.

'We're dreaming, Woody. We come out to Naples, conditioned by fear of its streetcrime. Perdita and her friends are warned to carry their mobiles and money under their sweatshirts – but that would make sense back in London. Jean and I stare up a back alley hung with washing-lines, and we think we're in the nostalgia scenes of *The Godfather*. If we hadn't scurried away, I still think we could have found the right loo handle for her bathroom – there was a promising shop full of chromeware, just before she decided people were giving us the evil eye . . .'

Though keen on the cavities behind lavatory tanks, Woody had no views on fitments. Mr Grubshaw enticed him back into the matchbox, for it was dinnertime.

Perhaps because Grubby thought he saw a limousine turning onto the causeway, they ate out below the Castel d'Ovo, where there were several good-class pizzerias. It was their last night, which they spent in happy talk of archaeology and food, while dodging the attentions of musicians. 'For the *bambina*!' leered a waiter, placing pasta before Jean, who blushed. Grubby walked outside 'to make a phonecall to the office'; flirting with an Italian waiter was just what Jean needed at this stage.

He stayed in sight in case she panicked, leaning on a

short harbour wall. A group of town dogs assembled around him, not begging, but sitting on their haunches in a circle as if they recognised a crony. People came and went in couples or groups. Then, oddly, a man alone walked up the shadowed cobbled street; he was short, chunky, had a mobile phone clamped to his ear. He looked like Renzo. A second figure followed him on lighter feet: peak-capped and blazered. Mr Grubshaw would have tailed them, but now Jean was gesticulating. Time to return to the restaurant.

They ate, settled up, bemoaned the end of their holiday. They took a turn around the little square and the dark quays at the foot of the fortress. Among the parked cars were none Grubby recognised, nor did he spot anyone familiar eating outside. Not that he expected to; they had observed that regulars were greeted specially by smiling maitre d's and wafted indoors to private rooms. 'With menus at half-price,' said Jean.

'Same the world over,' replied Grubby.

'These locals behave as if they own the joint.'

'Maybe they do, Jean.'

He slept badly, anxious to ensure they caught their flight. Rising early, he booked out, left his suitcase in the lobby where Jean and his niece would see it, then took a last constitutional along the esplanade. Braving traffic, he crossed the frantic Via Partenope to the shore. Joggers and anglers had gathered in a knot. Normally the fishermen sat on the great slabs of concrete that thrust skywards, as if heaved by volcanic upheaval. They formed a breakwater. There was no beach; the waves lapped imperceptibly against these jagged, jumbled chunks from which hopefuls cast rods every few yards.

Not today. On one of the massive slabs lay a body.

With his conscience pricking, Mr Grubshaw ascertained

that it was male. All he could see was dark clothing; he thought of Renzo, habitually in black jeans and a zipped black bomber jacket. 'A vagrant?' he queried discreetly, as the joggers and anglers stared and waited for the police.

'Most likely,' a man explained to him a little too carefully, 'someone who drank too much—' He mimed it. 'And fell from a cruise liner.'

'Not local, then!' said Grubby. His tone was wry.

A police car drew up and switched on its siren. Two officers clambered to the corpse while colleagues joked with bystanders. Soon the body was turned over. From the pavement, it was still impossible to identify the man or see how he died. The nearest policeman straightened up and began serious phoning on his mobile. An angler and a jogger exchanged glances. Mr Grubshaw decided to return to his hotel.

Perhaps troubled by what he had seen, his feet took him too far. He pulled up, outside the grander establishment beyond. A limousine was parked, its chauffeur in a blue blazer leaning on one door, picking his teeth. The man gave him a courteous 'Good morning' nod. On a whim, Grubby entered the hotel and was directed to its restaurant. At the window table a mature woman breakfasted alone. Waiters hovered near her, but she ignored them, mopping her mouth with a napkin as she gazed down outside, watching the kerfuffle on the shore. No expression showed on her face.

Mr Grubshaw glanced at his watch, made his excuses, and returned to his own hotel. Police activity had increased, an ambulance was now in attendance, and a senior officer was looking taut. There was no attempt to halt the traffic, but after he found his companions, getting cases into a taxi was safer than normal as drivers slowed down of their own accord to gape at the crime scene.

'She fixed him, then!'

'Now, Jean; you don't know that.'

At the airport, Mr Grubshaw craned for sightings of Renzo, without result.

All the following week, he checked the barber's shop, but it remained shuttered. He tackled Cursing Khaleed. 'Renzo gone away?'

'Effing Italy.'

'Business?'

''Oliday, he say. Was arrested at the effing airport for carrying a knife.'

'Bloody hell!' Khaleed looked offended by Mr Grubshaw's language. 'How d'you know, Khaleed?'

'Rang me on his mobile. I had to shift some stuff for him in case the effing cops search the shop.'

'What – he went over his allowance for duty-free after-shave?' White powder, more likely, Grubby thought.

'Somebody stitched him up, he say.'

'I was afraid somebody had done him in.'

'Just effing deported . . . Try Mario's, up Greenwich,' Khaleed advised, fingering his own sinister shaved head. 'Does an effing swanky cut. You going away? My cousin's got a nice apartment in Bodrum. Do you an effing good price.'

'Can't get away. Too many family commitments . . .' Clive was terrified of what Jean might have planned for him financially, and Jean was scaring herself with her hardened attitude. Even his niece, despite her insouciance, was starting to look pinched with worry. 'Thanks,' answered Grubby, 'but I think I'll stay at home this year.'

BETWEEN THE LINES

Colin Dexter

17 Bridgnorth Street
Kidderminster

10th August

Dear Ronald,

I was sittin' only a coupla feet away on the night Big Jimmy was shot through his underachieving brain . . .

That's my opening gambit. No – that *was* my opening gambit.

Remember how our guru gave us those three guidelines? First, grab 'em all with that first sentence of yours. Second, don't get too worried if you find yourself writing a load of crap. Third (this is it!), if you want a short cut to 'ideas', just take any situation you've experienced recently, doesn't matter how pedestrian and trite, write it up as quickly as you can, and then just change one of the incidents in it, just the *one*, and see how your story suddenly leaps into life.

So please read my entry (enclosed) for our competition. How I need that prize-money! There's not much 'grab' about the new opening, but plenty of 'crap' in the rest. I'm not bothered. It was that *third* guideline that stuck in my underachievin' brain, and you'll soon spot that one fictitious incident in the story. Forgive me! Here goes.

The Theft

There were twenty-three of us on that trip, with me the youngest but one. Mistakenly, I'd never expected things to live up to the brochure's promise: 'Ten days amid the cultural delight of Prague, Vienna and Budapest, with a unique mix of travel, guided tours and group seminars in creating writing. Travel is by rail, coach and boat. Each of our experienced guides is fluent in English. The leader of the seminar is himself a published author with four acclaimed novels to his name.'

I fell for him a bit from day one, and once or twice I thought he might be vaguely attracted to a single woman about ten years younger than he was. So I was disappointed when it was another man in the group who came to sit beside me as we travelled on the long train journey from Prague to Vienna. It happened like this.

The first-class carriage into which the group was booked was already uncomfortably full when the porter finally lugged my large, over-packed case up from the platform and told me it would have to be stowed away in the next carriage. No problem really. Since I was determined not to let my precious case out of my sight, I decided to leave the rest of the group and move along into the next carriage myself; and in truth I almost welcomed the thought of being alone and of concentrating my mind on that glittering short-story prize. I had already taken my seat and was reconsidering my opening sentence . . .

But I got no further.

'Mind if I join you?' (Did I?) 'I thought you'd probably be a bit lonely and—'

But before Ernest Roland, one of our group, had any chance of continuing, the automatic doors opened and two latish-middle-aged women made their way breathlessly into our comparatively empty carriage, each dragging a vast, wheeled case behind them. For a few seconds they stood beside us, glancing indecisively around, before pushing the two cases into the empty space on the carriage floor across the aisle, and finally settling down into the vacant twin-seats immediately in front of us, their backs towards us. From the window seat she had taken, it was the larger of the two ladies who spoke first: 'Well, we made it, Emily!'

Emily was a much slimmer, smaller-boned woman with a rather nervous-looking face – a face I could see quite clearly slantwise, for a slightly curious reason. Throughout the carriage the backs of the seats were designed in such a way that an opening was left running down the middle, fairly narrow at the top and the bottom, but with a bulbous swelling in the centre, some four to five inches wide, the whole gap shaped like an old-fashioned oil-lamp. From my seat therefore, also by the window, my view of her was pretty well unrestricted, as was the view of the broad adjustable arm-rest in black leather which separated the blue-upholstered seats. The whole design was light and airy: a comfortable arrangement for passengers' comfort, if not for passengers' privacy. Indeed, we could follow the newcomers' conversation quite clearly since each spoke English, albeit with an odd transatlantic twang that almost sounded *un*-American. Very soon we learned that the window-seated widow (?) was named Marion; and it was

Ernest who turned to me, eyebrows lifted, as he pointed
to Marion's chubby right hand on the arm-rest, the middle
finger displaying one of the largest solitaire diamonds I
have ever seen. And I was wondering what beautiful bril-
liants bedecked her other hand when the connecting doors
opened behind us. 'Listek, prosim.' Then with a change
of gear to a moderate semblance of English, 'Teekits,
please.'

Ernest managed to explain that we were both members
of the . . . he pointed back over his shoulder.

The ticket collector nodded and moved a pace forward.
'You English also as well?'

'No,' said Marion, 'we – are – from – Quebec – in Canada.
You understand?'

The man shook his head and both women were now
dipping their hands into their hand-luggage.

'Don't worry, dear,' said Emily.

But Marion's fingers continued to scrabble around the
bottom of her bag, trawling a collection of brochures, tour-
guides, papers, documents and whatever; and was placing
them all in a pile on the arm-rest beside her when Emily
gave a sotto-voce squeak of delight. '*I've* got them – *both
of them!*'

The man checked and clipped each ticket, and moved on
a few paces before turning round and eyeing the cases.

'Yours?'

'Yes.'

'I am sorry but . . .'

'You want them moved?' asked Marion belligerently.

'Next stopping per'aps many people . . .'

'We understand,' said Emily.

Ernest grinned at me: 'I think per'aps, er, we ought to . . .'

'So do I.'

We both stood up and joined Marion, who was already

out of her seat and staring fecklessly at the luggage when Ernest laid his hand gently on her shoulder.

'Why don't you sit down and relax. *I'll* move the cases to the luggage place at the end of the carriage. They'll be fine there – it's where my friend here has left hers.' He smiled sweetly; and Marion expressed her gratitude equally sweetly as she sat down again – as did I when Ernest insisted that he could manage well enough – better, in fact – without any help from me.

Quickly the cases were stowed; and with my companion back beside me I had no opportunity of developing a second dazzling sentence that would follow my daring murder of poor big Jimmy. In any case there was soon a further interruption.

Two uniformed Czech soldiers stood beside us, asking in good English to see our passports. Ernest and I were immediately cleared. As was Emily. But Marion was once again scrabbling away in her bag in a state of incipient panic.

'Don't worry, madam. We'll come back.'

They moved along the carriage, and a flushed-faced Marion turned to Emily. 'It's in my wallet. I *know* it is. But where *is* the wallet?'

'Didn't you see it when you were looking for your ticket, dear?'

'I just can't remember and then you found my ticket and . . . I'm going mad . . . I just—'

She broke off, very close to tears now as, for a second time, she began piling up the bag's contents on the arm-rest, and as a kneeling Emily was spreading her small hands over every square inch of the carpet around them. And we joined her. With no success.

'I had it when . . .' bemoaned Marion. 'I just wonder if . . . You know those sort of zip-up things on the side of my case? Yes! I'll just . . .'

She got up and walked to the luggage area, only to return almost immediately, her face betraying disappointment.

'Do you know exactly what else was in the wallet, Marion?'

'Not exactly.'

'How much money?'

'About a thousand euros – more, I should think.'

'As much as that?'

'You don't have to rub it in, Emily!'

A knight in shining armour now rode upon the scene in the form of a dark-suited middle-aged man who had been seated further along the carriage and who spoke excellent English, albeit with an obvious German accent. 'Excuse me for intruding, ladies. My name is Herr Steiner. I just wonder if I may be of some help to you?' He explained that he worked with the Canadian Consulate in Vienna, and that he couldn't help overhearing about the wallet, containing passport, money and (surely?) plastic cards as well. (Marion had nodded.) Above all the good lady should be worried about the cards, because even without a PIN number the thief would for a while have unlimited access to the big stores in the major cities.

For the first time Marion seemed aware of the full implications of her loss: 'I shall have to cancel the cards, yes.'

'That's where I can help you, if you wish it. You have a mobile phone?'

'My good friend here—'

'It's not charged, dear,' confessed a contrite Emily.

'Do you have any details about your passport number, card numbers . . .?'

Temporarily at ease, Marion produced the sheet of A4 which we had already observed on the arm-rest.

Herr Steiner perused the sheet carefully: 'My goodness!

Passport number, copy of your photo, card numbers – even your PIN number. You really shouldn't let anyone see *that*, you know. But it won't be difficult to sort out the passport and cancel the cards. And if you would like me to do it for you . . .?' The offer was gladly accepted; and very soon we heard Herr Steiner, back in his seat, reeling off strings of numbers in German into his mobile phone.

Ten minutes later all arrangements had been made: cards cancelled, and the address given of the consulate offices in Vienna. Herr Steiner was back in his seat resuming his reading of Heinrich Heine's biography. Marion and Emily were now conversing almost normally. Ernest and I were swapping our assessment of the tour so far, and promising to send each other a copy of our short-story entry.

After crossing the Czech-Austrian border, it came as no surprise that we were subjected to a further passport inspection with (we had been warned) the Austrian police somewhat more officious and perhaps a little more efficient than their Czech counterparts (who, incidentally, had not reappeared). The two men considered our passports carefully, like scrutineers at some electoral recount; then moved on to the Canadian travellers, and it was Herr Steiner who came forward and encored his guardian-angel act. He took the A4 sheet Marion handed to him and showed it to the policemen, itemising the information given in rapid yet quietly spoken German. After some note-taking, and some discussion, their faces impassive, the policemen passed on up the carriage and Herr Steiner translated their instructions to Emily and Marion: when the train reached its destination in Vienna, both of them must remain in the carriage where a station official would meet them.

And that was about it really. Well, no – it wasn't.

Just before we reached Vienna, our group leader came through to ask us to join the main party for a short briefing. Ernest fetched my case and the pair of us left the carriage, bidding farewell to the Canadian ladies, but not to Herr Steiner, who must have been temporarily elsewhere since Heinrich Heine was still lying on his seat.

And what of Marion's wallet? Well, it will perhaps surprise my readers to learn exactly what happened to it because I know the full truth of the matter.

It is easy enough to make a couple of intelligent guesses: first, that the wallet was not lost, but stolen; second, that the theft occurred on the train, and most probably in the very carriage in which Ernest and I found ourselves. Again, motives for the theft are variously obvious: in themselves passports are valuable items for much criminal chicanery, particularly for falsifying identities or legitimising bogus immigrations; the possession of other people's credit cards, especially with PIN numbers presented on a plate, can be extremely profitable – at least in the short term; and the attraction of a thick wodge of banknotes . . . Need I say more?

But *who* was the guilty party in all this?

Plenty of suspects. The Czech police would be the obvious ones, since anyone finding the wallet would probably give it to them, and they were on the scene from the start. The Austrian police? If they'd had little opportunity of finding the wallet itself, they'd had ample time to note down its key contents, so obligingly set forth on the sheet Marion had handed them. But why, if they were the guilty party, did they bother to arrange a meeting with a 'station official' in Vienna? If, in fact, they *had* done so . . .

But no! Cross all four off the list, as well as the ticket collector – no, I'd not forgotten him! I know that in detective stories it is frequently the unlikeliest who turn out to be the crooks; but in real life it is usually the *like-liest*; and for me it was that smoothie of a 'diplomat' (ha!) who had moved into the top spot. Was it really necessary for him to spend so long studying Marion's sheet when he'd phoned – if in truth he was talking to *anyone*? And where was he when he left the carriage? Not in the toilet or the buffet-car because he would have had to pass us if he'd visited either. And he didn't. And incidentally, *he* wasn't the thief either.

So what we needed was a sharply observant detective, like Poirot, say – or someone like me. For *I* was the one who had observed the thief bend down to pick up a deliberately dropped Vienna guide from the dark blue carpet at the side of the aisle; and to pick up something else at the same time – the semi-camouflaged wallet, also dark blue, and casually to slip both items into what he called his Fisherman's Bag. That person was Ernest, my companion.

How he profited from his theft I do not know, and have little desire to know. But it was a sad day for me when he came to sit beside me on that journey. The saddest recollection of all, though, is a small thing, yet one I always shall remember. As the train was slowing down at the outskirts of Vienna, Emily got down on her knees and felt along the whole of the carpet once more. I could have – should have – told the poor old dear that she was wasting her time. But I didn't.

Finis

Well, there it is, Ronald. Sorry I couldn't think of a decent anagram of your Christian name: 'Roland' is far too weak. But your surname came to the rescue, tho' I've never been too fond of 'Ernest'. Do read the story and let me know what you think.

Fond regards,
Diana (Duncan-Jones)
P.S. No Brownie points for guessing the 'one
incident' that's been changed!

29 Emmanuel Road
Cambridge

14th August

Dear Diana,

Thank you for your story – much enjoyed –
although the last two paragraphs were a bit painful
to tell you the truth. I understand why you had no
joy in trying to anagram Ronald but I trust I've done
better with you! I haven't got your skill as a writer
since (until your dénouement) you describe the
sequence of events with accuracy and economy and
you quite certainly took our leader's injunction to
heart about just changing one of the incidents. I've
decided not to enter the competition myself but I've
girded my loins and written an ending which relates
far more closely to the truth. Ready? I begin with 'So
what we needed . . .'

So what we needed was a sharply observant
detective, like Poirot, say – or someone like me!
For I was the one who had noticed Nadia bend
down on the pretext of retrieving a deliberately
dropped guide-book and picking up the wallet
with it and nonchalantly slipping both into her
capacious handbag. I cannot believe she was
sufficiently street-wise to understand the full

potential of the wallet's contents. But I do know (she had told me on the tour) that she was getting uncomfortably short of ready monies. How she profited from her theft I have no desire to know but it was a sad day for me when I went through to join her on our railway journey. I said nothing to Nadia of course since I felt a keen distaste for the bloated Marion who looked as if she'd been stuffing her stomach with the most expensive meals in the most expensive restaurants in Prague – probably at the expense of the emaciated Emily.

Finis

Now listen Diana! For *me* the saddest thing of all is that we should both have come out of this with our reputations tarnished at least on the printed page since clearly neither of us has a particularly high opinion of the other. I must admit though that I took a bit of a shine to you and I think I still would have but for our time on the train together. What a pity things have ended like this! I shall put pen to paper no more about that strange morning since I am not such a big fan as you are of the 'changed incident' guidelines. But as you will have noticed I *have* changed just that *one* little thing: I did not actually see you pick up the wallet. I *did* however see the wallet in your handbag and I *did* see you push it down deeper so that it was no longer visible.

On a final and more constructive note let me congratulate you on your much more economical use of dashes and let me congratulate myself on using not a single comma in this letter to you.

Ronald Sterne

Extract From a Diary

Feb 5th 2005

I've only a few weeks to live, they tell me, and tho' I
was brought up as an R.C. I've never been into a
confessional to tell of the sins I've committed. In any
case I've no real regrets for any of them. My only
confidante in life has been you, dear diary, and this
will almost certainly be my last entry.

Marion and I were in the same class in secondary
school; but after leaving we had exchanged only a
few perfunctory letters over the years. So it came as
a surprise when she wrote to me early last year
informing me that her (second!) husband, a big wig
with BA, had died, and inviting me, a lifelong spin-
ster, to join her on a fortnight's Hapsburg Holiday,
dividing our time between Prague, Vienna and
Budapest. An additional carrot was Marion's
promise of an upgrade to Club Class (thanks to her
late husband), and it was that which swayed me. I
felt fairly sure that I could, in spite of my deterio-
rating health, just about cope with the travel, and
almost everything else really – and I accepted the
invitation.

Marion had always been a big and bouncy and
bullying girl at school, and I had been hurt deeply (we
were both seventeen) when she had robbed me of the
only boyfriend I've ever had in my life, one of the
sixth-formers a year ahead of us: Jonathan. And it took
a very short time for me to realise that her boisterous
nature had blossomed over the years (thirty-five of
them) and developed into a selfish bossiness that I
found well-nigh intolerable on occasions. Increasingly I

found I had no real say about where we went, what we ate, at what time we did whatever she'd decided to do. I won't go on.

At one point tho' things did become intolerable.

Many times when we were sitting together over a meal or over drinks, we spoke of our school days; and the evening before we were to catch our train from Prague to Vienna she asked me a question quite out of the blue.

'Did you ever keep in touch with Jonathan?'

'No.'

'He was very sweet on you, you know.'

'Not as sweet as he was on you.'

'I don't know about that. After you'd left school and gone off to Shropshire – and after things had cooled down between us—'

'Yes?'

'He asked me if I had your new address.'

'Which you did have.'

'Of course. But he would have been no good for you, Emily dear.'

'Did you give him my address?'

'No, I didn't. He was a bit of a wimp, you know, and I thought you'd got over him by then – like I had.'

'Don't you think that what *I* thought was more important than what *you* thought?'

'To be truthful, Emily, I don't, no.'

That was it – virtually verbatim, I swear it. I didn't want to murder Marion, not quite, but I desperately wanted to hurt her. How? I'd no real idea, but someone was smiling down on me the morning we boarded the Vienna-bound train.

Seated immediately behind us were two youngish things on a group holiday; he, Ronald by name (we could hear all they said) seemed a pleasant enough fellow, with a quietly diffident manner, in sharp contrast to his companion, named Diana, who sounded a selfish little bitch, openly flirting with her beau and equally openly bemoaning her shortage of cash. But both of them got up to help Marion when the ticket-man told us to move our luggage. So I was left alone for a couple of minutes, and all I needed was a couple of seconds. My opportunity! I took Marion's wallet from her bag and through the gap at the back of our seats I pushed it down into Diana's open hand-luggage. A lightning impulse and so risky. If the girl had told us of her great surprise at finding the wallet in her bag, who could have done the deed – except me? And I have never in my life felt so relieved as when we finally reached Vienna without her saying a word about the matter.

Marion soon bounced back of course from this slightly distressing experience. The station official at Vienna was charming and helpful; the consulate had already made arrangements for the passport, all cards had been cancelled; the insurance company later coughed up not only for the euros but even for the wallet. This last information I learned when she rang me a few weeks later, but we have not communicated since. My one remaining hope is that she will not hear of my death and turn up to shed a perfunctory tear at my funeral. But I mustn't be too hard on her. At least I enjoyed flying Club Class.

Just one thing I'm vaguely curious about: I wonder whether Diana and Ronald kept in touch after they reached home, and if so what they said to each other.

At least *he* would have had knowledge of her address, surely so – which, alas, is more than Jonathan had of mine.

THE LIFE-LIE

Robert Barnard

'It's going to be a hard couple of days,' said Einar Høgset. Arnoldus Fossli simply shrugged. 'One might have hoped that age had mellowed him, but . . .' Høgset went on, gesturing at a pile of newspapers.

'*Verdensgang*,' said Fossli bitterly. 'The Way of the World. If *this* is the way the press is leading us, God help us.'

'Perhaps it is not leading us, but following. The appetite for sensational stories about prominent people seems to be universal nowadays.'

'Maybe. And perhaps he has behaved badly. But didn't he have cause? The world's greatest dramatist on a seventieth-birthday tour of honour to Copenhagen, the gastronomic capital of Scandinavia, and what do they offer him? Two sandwiches and a bottle of schnapps.'

'It shows a terrible lack of sophistication,' agreed Høgset. 'And Stockholm was no better.'

'To address him at a formal dinner as "du" – the familiar form! The whole world knows he expects "de" except from close friends.'

'Of whom there are remarkably few. Yes, it's no wonder he marched straight out of the hall . . . We in Bergen will do much better in both respects.'

'True,' said Fossli. 'Because we have been warned – by

Verdensgang. But remember, there must be millions of other ways of offending, irritating, or insulting Herr Ibsen. And most of those we have not been forewarned about. The possibilities for disaster are endless.' He looked around the cavernous spaces of the Hotel Bristol, as if to get a warning on other potential pitfalls during the impending visit, but no inspiration struck.

'Well, we have reserved the best suite in the best hotel in Bergen, and the banquet will serve the best fish in a wonderful new recipe named after his greatest heroine, Nora. What more could we do?'

'That we shall probably find out,' said Høgset drily. 'Come – we'd better go to the station. He will be here in twenty minutes' time.'

'I shall walk to clear my head.'

Høgset nodded. His own open carriage was waiting outside in the street. He was a ship owner, and he believed that his position as one of Bergen's richest men depended on the messages he sent out to the hoi-polloi. He did things in style – always, in every respect. Nothing, if he could help it, was to mar the visit of Herr Ibsen. It was to be the high-point, the glory, of his period of office as mayor.

The five-minute walk to the station brushed away the cobwebs from Herr Fossli's brain, but offered him no illumination of possible future dangers that could be circumvented. At the station he surveyed the modest streamers of welcome to the man who had once been in effect the director of the town's theatre company, then joined the party of notables gathered, no doubt on the station-master's instructions, a short way up the platform.

Høgset nodded to him, but nobody said anything. If it had been King Oscar there would have been some conversation, but for Herr Ibsen there was only a tense silence. Everyone was terrified.

On time to the minute, the train from Voss steamed merrily into the station. Herr Ibsen had been resting in the mountains and superintending the arrival of spring. Seated in the compartment which drew neatly up beside the reception committee was the man they had come to meet and honour. He had a large head, emphasised by the unruly halo of white and grey hair. His mouth was a small, unyielding line, also surrounded by hair, but the men on the platform waiting were mainly transfixed by the eyes. It was as if one was large and one was small: the latter was quiescent and good-humoured, while the other, large one was spraying sparks of contradiction, malice and ire. As the other travellers began to disembark the important visitor sat still, unblinking, as if posing for one of the innumerable paintings and busts of himself that were currently being produced for the seventieth birthday.

'I think he expects us to go to his compartment,' murmured Høgset. 'Perhaps Herr Fossli and I—?'

There was no jealous murmur from the rest, only a silent sigh of relief, possibly observed by the malicious great eye from the train. Høgset and Fossli boarded the train, reached the Great Man's compartment, and bowed their greeting.

'Welcome back to Bergen, Herr Ibsen,' Høgset said. Herr Ibsen immediately got up, revealing a smallish body with delicate hands and feet, surmounted by that mop of grizzled hair and the monstrous eye.

'Thank you, thank you,' he said, leading the way and gesturing to his suitcase and bags on the rack, confident they would be seen to. At the door he surveyed the waiting notables.

'You are very kind,' he murmured, each word prissily and distinctly enunciated. 'Will you excuse me if I do not shake hands with you all? After my visits to Copenhagen and Stockholm my right hand is suffering from overuse.'

He waved a swollen paw, then suffered himself to be led through the station and out to Herr Høgset's carriage, the fine white horses to draw which were champing discontentedly in the street. Herr Ibsen looked at the sparkling scene, then up towards the sun.

'It is never sunny in Bergen,' he said. 'How is it you have not arranged the usual rain for me?'

'Perhaps we thought you had given *us* enough rain in your *Ghosts*,' said Fossli, greatly daring. It was, after all the only Ibsen play he had seen, attracted by the rumour that it was a 'dirty play'. He was rewarded with a chuckle.

The people of Bergen going about their daily business stopped and waved or cheered as the carriage clip-clopped – slowly, by order – around the lake and towards the Hotel Bristol. Ibsen kept looking around him, trying to take in the lie of the town.

'It is so different, so changed,' he said. The word *forandret* was beautifully enunciated, each sound elongated. Neither man was sure whether he meant it was changed for the better or worse, but he removed doubt by adding 'And still so beautiful.' There was another sigh of relief, and that too was probably observed by that most observing of men.

At the Hotel Bristol the staff were lined up in order of importance from the street door to the Grand Staircase. Herr Ibsen nodded as he came through the door, then paid the lines of honour no more attention. As so often when respect was shown to him he seemed torn between pleasure at his own celebrity and consciousness that he was renowned as a fighter against hypocrisy and pretension. When the trio had gained his suite, which was adorned with a large if mass-produced portrait of King Oscar, who had stayed in it, his eyes went round the room, a near-smile played on his lips, and he turned to Høgset and Fossli.

'We had nothing like this in Bergen in my day,' he said. 'Thank you. And now I am tired. I must rest and take a bath.'

'If we may we will call on you to take you down to the banquet,' said Mayor Høgset. 'This is Bergen, so we shall have some very fine fish.'

The smile on Ibsen's face became a wicked one.

'I am happy with a sandwich and a bottle of schnapps, if the spirit of hospitality is there,' he said. Then he sat down in an armchair and closed his eyes, the large one last. Høgset and Fossli tiptoed out.

'Phew!' Høgset said. 'I can't believe how well it is going.'

'Too well,' said Fossli.

'Hmmm. We shall see. I am accustomed to keeping things on an even keel. I look forward to seeing you and your lady wife tonight. Best bib and tucker, tell her.'

'My wife intends to wear her *bunad*,' said Fossli.

'Ohhh. National costume is all very well, but Herr Ibsen is an international figure and this is an international occasion . . . Oh well, women won't be told, will they?'

'I shouldn't say that in Herr Ibsen's hearing,' said Fossli.

While Høgset went out to his carriage, Fossli lingered at the reception desk to check that the last undecided details of the banquet's courses and seating arrangements had now been satisfactorily settled. Then he walked out into Markeveien.

'Hei, Mishter! Got a few øre for a poor chap?'

It was a drunk, a feature of Bergen after two o'clock. Herr Fossli turned towards Torgalmenning.

'Hei, you're one of the knobsh, aren't you? Hobnobbing with the great Ibsen? Itsh your great day, ishn't it? Guesh you could spare a krone for a glash of schnapps.'

The accent was not Bergen. Fossli thought it was odd. Drunks in Norway usually kept to their home beats. He turned and looked at the man: red-faced, bleary-eyed, dirty.

The face was unknown to him, yet somehow familiar. The small, straight mouth . . .

'What is your name, my man?'

'Your man? You recognise me, don't you?'

'I've never seen you in my life. I asked your name.'

'Whatsh my name? I'll tell you. Itsh Henriksen. What else, eh? Eh? What else would it be?' And he held out his hand.

The import of the question struck Fossli like a wet haddock. He stopped, fumbled in his pocket, then drew out an overgenerous number of kroner.

'Five kroner,' crowed the man. 'Itsh what he gave me. Said it was what he gave my mother.'

The wet haddock came back from another blow across the other cheek. Fossli paused for a moment, then turned and hurried back into the hotel.

'I have to use your telephone,' he said.

The Bristol was the only hotel in Bergen to have a telephone. Einar Høgset was one of hardly more than a dozen private subscribers, which gave him great prestige but a limited list of conversationalists. Høgset was not yet home, so Fossli spoke to the man who would be a butler if Norway had butlers, but who was called by Høgset his head of staff.

'Something extremely important has come up,' Fossli said. 'I need to talk to Herr Høgset urgently and in private. Perhaps he could call round at my home on his way to the banquet. Or, better still, immediately. I shall be at home in five minutes. Please stress that it is of the utmost importance.'

Then he went to his corn chandler's store, above which his home occupied two floors. Fossli belonged to the cultured mercantile class in Bergen, whereas Høgset belonged by marriage to the uncultured shipowning class. Arnoldus Fossli always thought his superior reading gave him a slight edge, enabling him to shrug at Høgset's flourished proofs of his superior wealth. He also occasionally mentioned to intimates that Høgset's wealth came entirely from marriage and arse-licking.

He heard the arrival of the mayor's carriage ten minutes later, and hurried his wife off to the kitchen. 'No listening,' he ordered. When the bell rang he ushered Høgset into his business office, and told him of the encounter outside the Bristol.

'When I asked his name—'

'Why did you do that? Of some common-or-garden tramp?'

'Because there was something about his face. His accent. He came from East Norway. We don't export our drunks from town to town in this country. And when I asked my question he looked at me and said, "Henriksen. What else?"'

'What could he mean by—? . . . Oh, my God.'

'Yes. Son of Henrik. The son he had in Grimstad when he was about eighteen. By some kitchen maid or other. The drunk who rolls about Christiania boasting about his paternity. Actually went and cadged money off him once, so they say.'

'Five kroner,' said Høgset wonderingly.

'By an odd chance I gave him the same. And he said, "It's what he gave me." And apparently what he gave the mother too. So all the stories are true.'

'Or this drunk made up the stories and now believes them,' said Høgset. 'He's here to cause trouble.'

'How on earth did he get here? The boat fare would be beyond him.'

'Who knows? Perhaps some kind man in Christiania gave him the ticket. They have no love for us there.'

'Or for him either.'

'Leave it to me!' said Høgset, as if inspiration had struck. 'Do nothing, above all *say* nothing, not to your wife, not to anyone. I'll see you in the Bristol fifteen minutes before the banquet.'

And he marched off with the sublime confidence of a man who has spent his life solving tricky problems, or thinks he has. Fossli was troubled. He went to the kitchen to find his wife, now resplendent in her *bunad*.

'Would you mind if we didn't go to the banquet together?' he asked her. 'Could you go along with Fru Lysne or Fru Ryall?'

She shrugged.

'Of course. Or I can go on my own. I have a great desire to see the Great Man but no desire to get near him to make conversation with him.'

So that was all right. Arnoldus Fossli dressed himself quickly in full evening rig, brushed his hair over the bald expanses of his head, and left the house. It was not exactly that he distrusted Einar Høgset, but he did have the feeling that the man's judgement was not quite as good as he thought it was. And this feeling was accentuated when he arrived in Torgalmenning and saw Høgset at the other end of its wide space.

He was already dressed for the banquet. He was talking to a figure whom Fossli recognised as one of the town's drunks – someone who had been up before him (and doubtless before Høgset) many times when they sat as magistrates. He saw Høgset reach into his pocket and take out money. He turned, shaking his head, and made towards Markevei and the Bristol.

The idea was all right: to give one drunk enough to get two drunks incapable, with the proviso that he take the newcomer from Eastern Norway off somewhere and make sure that the rest of Ibsen's visit was free from embarrassment (he was to leave by the next morning's steamer for Stavanger). It was the detail that concealed the devil: to do it in daylight, in evening dress, in the centre of town, to make it obvious that money was changing hands. Everyone in Bergen knew that Høgset, before becoming mayor or since, was not a man to give good money to a drunk.

But when Høgset arrived at the Bristol he was in high good humour, and together they went up to Herr Ibsen's room without fear. The Great Man was already clad in evening dress, which made him look as if he were buttoned up in stiff cardboard, and on his chest he wore the Grand Cross of the Northern Star, recently awarded him in Stockholm by King Oscar. It was perhaps this (for he was known to value such distinctions well beyond their merits) that had kept him in high good humour.

There was to be no high table, no raised-dais affair, with one line of diners very visible from the floor of the hall. This was by order of Herr Ibsen: the man who could flaunt his latest bauble was a mass of contradictions and forbade any singling-out. Thus he entered the banqueting hall of the hotel to great applause, which he acknowledged by several blinks of the eye, then he walked through the assembled people of Bergen flanked by Høgset and Fossli till he came to their table by the windows and his place in the centre facing the other tables. As they sat down Høgset introduced the other notables:

'Herr Lie, our city treasurer and Fru Lie, Herr Høydahlsvik, our director of education, Herr Østergård, our secretary of commerce . . .' and so on until he came to the young lady whose place was opposite Herr Ibsen. 'And I have taken the liberty to place my daughter Anne-Lise opposite you, which is to her a great honour, as you can imagine.'

Herr Ibsen's partiality for young girls – plump, charming,

admiring – was well known, and hosts who acknowledged this preference, instead of filling every spare place with boring local placemen, enjoyed the full sun of his favour. Arnoldus Fossli had never seen the mayor's daughter before, though he had known his late wife, whom Høgset had married for her ships. Fossli wondered if this young miss was the Great Man's type of girl. There was, behind the girlish mannerisms, a steely sparkle to the eyes that to him suggested a single-minded stupidity. Was the stupidity an inheritance from her mother? Or was the combination of single-mindedness and stupidity, conceivably, a link with her father?

She started in as soon as Herr Ibsen, after greeting her, had sat down.

'You must be wondering why a seventeen-year-old is in a place of honour like this, Herr Ibsen, but Mama died several years ago and I'm going to take her place as the mayor's lady, and I couldn't have a more wonderful baptism in the role than this dinner to honour someone who has done so much for women in this country, everybody says so, and even I can see it's true. I read *Rasmusholm* last night and of course everyone knows about Nora and slamming the door and all that, it's so wonderful your coming to Bergen because really Bergen *is* the heart of Norway, not Christiania, which Papa says is just a mushroom city with no history – oh dear, that's Papa on the job as always, they never stop badgering him for one reason or another—'

Herr Ibsen's eyes, which had glazed over, now turned to Einar Høgset seated two places down from his over-confident daughter. An official of some kind had tapped him on the shoulder, and was now whispering in his ear. After a brief report from his underling, Høgset gave a few short orders and turned back to his *gravlaks*.

'Just a disturbance out of Sandviken – some of the local drunks.'

'Isn't it dreadful,' Anne-Lise began at once, 'how these people disgrace the name of Norway? Why do they drink? Here we are in the most beautiful country in the world and all they can think of is akevitt and beer and—'

On she went, and Herr Ibsen sighed and turned his attention to the *kveite Nora* which had replaced the salmon. Arnoldus Fossli registered the mayor's first unquestionable miscalculation of the evening.

'Shall I—?' he whispered.

'Shut her up? No, no. It allows us to think our thoughts. I have a feeling that Herr – Høgset is it? – will have only a brief period of duty as mayor.'

However that might be, some forty-five minutes into the banquet the official tapped once again the mayoral shoulder and had a further consultation. This time faces were grave. But when he had taken himself off, Høgset turned an apologetic face to his guest.

'Nothing to worry about, Herr Ibsen. A drunk has been fished out of the fjord. These things happen all the time, though he's not a local. I doubt we'll find out how he got there. If he was pushed, the man who did it probably won't remember. I apologise for the interruption, Herr Ibsen. I like to be kept informed about everything that happens in the town.'

'Obviously,' muttered Ibsen under his breath.

When the *kalvefilet Oscar* had come and gone, and before the desserts and the coffee, the moment arrived for the speeches. This time, once again, the Great Man had put his foot down. The awful experience in Stockholm of being addressed with tipsy familiarity by a local notable was not to be repeated. He would be welcomed and introduced in a speech of not more than two minutes, after which he would reply in a speech of not more than ten minutes. A splendid fob watch had been laboriously unbuttoned from the depths of his waistcoat and now lay before him on the table.

At least he was being introduced by Høgset and not by his daughter. After two minutes of innocuous introduction, written for him by one of the Town Hall secretaries who had seen a couple of the plays, the mayor handed over, amid polite applause, to the Great Man. The large, searching, irritable eye and the softer, more friendly eye surveyed the massed tables of diners. Inevitably it was the fierce eye that everyone noted.

'My dear friends from Bergen!' Why did the tone of voice belie the words, making them sound more like a threat than a greeting? It was well known that there was a wonderful harmony of opinion between Norwegians and Herr Ibsen: he didn't much like them and they didn't much like him. 'My heart is full to be back with you, in the most beautiful of Norwegian towns. And it is full of memories and of questions too. How could the trustees of the Bergen theatre – the Nationale Scene you called it, confident that *you* were the nation! – How could they, back in 1851, have been so foolhardy or far-sighted (choose the word you prefer) as to entrust your theatre to a mere boy from the wrong side of Norway, who hardly knew more of plays and stagecraft than he knew of steam locomotion or the theory of gravity? What daring they showed, and how little, perhaps, I justified their faith.'

'I'm sure you did your best,' came from Anne-Lise Høgset.

Herr Ibsen's voice became louder and sharper, his enunciation more distinct and aggressive.

'But the best of a young sprig who had tried his hand at writing plays, writing drama criticism, was not enough. Here was I – producer, writer, dramaturg, dogsbody – the man who was thought to be able to do everything, but who could in fact do nothing properly. Except learn.'

'You certainly did that,' perkily observed Froken Høgset. Ibsen turned on her a look of undisguised contempt.

'Perhaps, my dear young lady, you will allow me the floor which you have graced for the length of this splendid meal.' Her mouth opened and shut like a fish's. 'And I learnt drama, I learnt about acting and scene-painting and scene-shifting. But I also learnt about life. Here I was, in a bustling cosmopolitan, moneymaking port. I had here my Peer Gynt (definitely a West Norwegian), my Stockmann, my Pastor Manders. Here were people making money, by fair means or foul. Here were people with prosperous exteriors, lavish lifestyles, but with inner corruption. Here I learnt what it is—' and here he seemed to look at Einar Høgset— 'to live a lie. "Take away a man's life-lie," one of my characters says, "and you rob him of his happiness." But sometimes it must be done. If I see a house which is built on rotten foundations – on crumbling earth, on sand or marshlands – I can prop it up, but only for so long. In the end I must move away and build a house on good earth. And that is what I learnt in Bergen. And what I have tried to say to the world. Because the corruption, hypocrisy, self-delusion is world-wide, part of our nineteenth-century civilisation. And the first spots of them, the symptoms of them, I saw here in Bergen forty years ago. Thank you.'

He sat down. The applause was lukewarm, not surprisingly. Suddenly he looked at Høgset and Fossli and beckoned, then got up and began walking towards the door. They managed to get on either side of him and make it look as if it had been scheduled. Some hardy souls managed to keep the applause going until he had made his way out through the doors and into the hotel foyer. He walked over to a dark corner, registered the hush from the banqueting hall, then turned fiercely on the two men, his cheeks bursting with outrage.

'And now, will you both please tell me what you have been doing?'

Høgset went red with embarrassment or anger, Fossli shuffled.

'Doing, Herr Ibsen?' prevaricated the mayor.

'You have been doing something, either separately or together. Let me tell you, since you both seem ignorant to the fact, that the Royal Suite here in the Bristol is on the corner of Markevei and Torgalmenning, and its windows look out on both thoroughfares.' Herr Fossli found it difficult to hide his apprehension at the direction the conversation was taking. 'So therefore I can see and do see, if Herr Fossli talks to a tramp in Markevei – a tramp whom I recognise and who was doubtless sent to Bergen by some ill-wisher – of mine, not of his. So let us assume that Herr Fossli learns that the drunk outside the hotel is claiming to be a bastard son of mine, and he scuttles back into the hotel. Why does he do that? Well, the hotel has a telephone, does it not? So he arranges a meeting with his superior, the mayor. So what happens next?'

'Herr Fossli knows nothing of what happened next,' said Høgset, who seemed to have misunderstood the situation so badly that he was anxious to claim all the credit.

'No doubt. You are a man who likes responsibility, I can see that. So you, on your own responsibility, arrange, via one of your underlings, a meeting with one of the town's tramps. And – what? – you get him to agree to get this supposed son of mine away from the town centre until I am safely out of the way and cannot be embarrassed while I am this fine town's guest. An excellent plan. You reward him in advance and – *what*? What else did you agree, or suggest?'

Like his daughter, Høgset opened and shut his mouth, suddenly understanding that things were not going his way.

'Did you tell him that it wouldn't worry you if an accident were to happen? That you would make sure that no harm would come to him, if that were the outcome of the night's work? Or did you go still further, and hint that an additional sum would be paid if that *was* the result of the evening rendezvous? And were you then aiming to present yourself to me as the man who, after an unfortunate accident, had hushed things up in an efficient and sympathetic manner so that there would be no unpleasant publicity for myself, on this auspicious anniversary?'

'Nothing of the s—' began Høgset.

'Are you, in fact, the sort of man who cultivates important people, marries into money and power, does the rich people's dirty work and reaps the rewards? I think so. And I think Herr Fossli has been dragged unwittingly along with your plans. I can do nothing. I have not an atom of proof. But you will gain nothing in prestige or power from what you have done. I feel no gratitude, only disgust. I trust I shall never see either of you again. I require no party to see me off in the morning. Goodbye.'

He turned and walked towards the stairs. Fossli, unable to look at Høgset, himself walked swiftly to the door. When he had reached it he paused for a moment to look back. Høgset was disappearing through the door to the banqueting hall, no doubt to put a brave face on the Great Man's snub to the people of Bergen. But, looking up, Fossli saw the figure of the Great Man himself, tightly buttoned still in his evening dress, going up the fine, broad staircase. He thought about the five kroner Ibsen had given his son, and still more about the five kroner he had given the boy's mother, and he thought that no one in his audience, not even Mayor Høgset, was hugging to his breast a more tawdry life-lie than the great dramatist himself.

Then he turned and went out into the darkened streets of the town.

Author's Note: *Quite a lot in this story is true, truish or conceivable, but not the plot. Hans Jacob Henriksen died ten years after his father in 1916, after a life filled with alcohol, wives, reading and the violin.*

THE WOMAN FROM MARLOW

Margaret Yorke

It was cold in the small church. Patrick wondered why Lance had suggested it for their meeting; why not a pub, where it would be warm? However, always curious, he took a descriptive pamphlet from a rack near the door, put his payment in the box provided, and consulted it as he wandered round. Building it was a remarkable achievement on the part of its Catholic-convert founder, subsequently endorsed by the addition of a modern extension to cater for the growing congregation. In the present godless age, this was impressive.

The door opened, and Lancelot Scott, eminent historian and former colleague of Patrick's at St Mark's College, Oxford, entered. He was a tall, angular man with snow-white curly hair cut very short. He appeared frequently on television and in radio debates, giving firm opinions on a wide range of subjects.

'Ha, Patrick,' he said. 'You found this place.'

'It wasn't difficult,' said Patrick drily. 'But why here?'

'I thought it would interest you if you were early,' said Lancelot. Patrick was known for his extreme punctuality.

'It does,' said Patrick.

'Well, you can finish reading about it later,' said Lancelot.

'Sit down and listen to what I have to tell you. It's quiet here, and we won't be overheard.'

'Unless another sightseer or some worthy soul who tends the church appears.'

Lancelot ignored this.

'I have a goddaughter, Amy, whose mother died recently,' he said. 'She had been suffering from dementia and it was extremely sad, as these cases are. I went to the funeral, of course, to support Amy.' He coughed, then added, 'I was very fond of Louise – her mother.'

'And the father?' asked Patrick, when Lance did not immediately continue his tale.

'Brian ran a family business. Biscuits. They were bought out by a bigger company years ago – did very well out of it – lovely house in the Cotswolds. They travelled a lot after that – had a house in Provence – and Brian did the country things, magistrate and so on. He owned a racehorse for a while.'

'A happy life?'

Lancelot shrugged, or was it more of a shiver? Patrick glanced at him sharply. Lancelot was not looking at him but staring ahead at the Pugin altar.

'It seemed so. Everyone thought them the ideal couple. Louise was a wonderful cook and hostess. Beautiful.' Lancelot's long, thin face seemed to become even longer and thinner as he spoke. 'Two children – a son, Hugh, and Amy. Hugh is a city broker.'

'And Amy?'

'Married to a farmer. Nice chap. Four children,' said Lancelot, and was it envy in his voice?

A wave of fellow feeling swept over Patrick. They were both bachelors, but not from choice. Patrick had always suspected that Lancelot had been carrying a torch for some woman – was it this Louise? – for much of his life. They had both buried themselves in academic life, with occasional emotional flurries when bold enough to pursue them. Patrick banished thoughts of Elizabeth, who was still alive and well. And, he earnestly hoped, happy.

'It seems that a few weeks before Louise died, Brian imported a woman into the house to look after her,' Lancelot continued. 'He said she was a school friend of Louise's, now a widow and lonely, and that they had all met socially when they were younger but had rather lost touch.'

'How had they resumed touch now?'

'That's what's concerned Amy,' said Lancelot. 'She didn't think this woman – her unlikely name is Marigold – was at school with Louise and she didn't think the two were friends. She was so worried that she rang me about it. She thinks Brian found Marigold on an Internet dateline.' As he uttered the words, Lancelot really did shudder. 'Brian was under a lot of strain. He has always been an impatient man, and it was difficult for him to cope with the changes in Louise, but after Marigold moved in he sacked the carer Amy had found only a few weeks earlier, saying it was better for Louise to have someone she knew. Louise was past knowing anyone by then, though she was always gentle and patient.'

Each time Lancelot had been to see her during her illness, she had always smiled, been warm and friendly, clearly knew he was someone she liked, but not who he was. The real Louise had been lost.

'Amy thought her mother was afraid of Marigold. She'd seen Louise shrink away from her when Marigold didn't realise that Amy was coming into the room,' he said.

'Amy lives near them?'

'About twenty miles away. She often went over and she offered to have Louise to live with them but Brian wouldn't agree. Said she liked her home and her familiar things. After Amy told me all this, I went to see Louise,' said Lancelot. 'I wanted to meet this Marigold. I didn't announce myself. I knew Louise never went anywhere unless Amy took her out. If I'd rung up, Brian might have tried to put me off – he'd say Louise was too tired for visitors or some other excuse.' He paused, still not looking at Patrick, before going on. 'I went one afternoon. I suppose I'd subconsciously planned what in fact I did, though I told myself I intended to ring the doorbell and wait to be admitted, but I knew if Louise was there on her own she might not answer.'

'You didn't ring? You slunk in?'

'Yes. Though Brian's car was outside the house, so he was around. The front door was locked but the back door was open. Louise spent the day in the small sitting room; I could hear the television on as I went past the door towards the front of the house. They weren't even upstairs. They were in the drawing room on the sofa. The door was half open. Anyone might have found them.'

'That was part of it, part of the thrill,' said Patrick, almost to himself.

'What?'

'The risk. But never mind. Go on,' said Patrick.

'I didn't confront them, if that's what you're wondering,' said Lancelot. He had felt physically sick as he retreated into the passage. 'If I'd looked in through the window I wouldn't have seen them, because of how the sofa was placed. Amy has a key to the house but she wouldn't have come unexpectedly then because she'd have been collecting her children from school. I went out again – slunk out – and drove away. Half an hour later I telephoned and said, very calmly, that I was passing and might I call in. Brian didn't sound too pleased but he agreed. He said Louise had deteriorated since my last visit and not to expect much from her. He spoke so coldly about her.'

Patrick nodded, though Lancelot, reliving the moment, did not notice.

'I wanted to see her face,' he said. 'That woman's. I wanted to be able to recognise her.'

'So what is she like?'

'She's very ugly,' said Lancelot. 'About six feet tall, with hair dyed a curious colour, sort of orange. Almost marigold, like her name, if it is her name. And dirty. She looked unwashed. Brian was looking bright and perky.'

'Fresh from the shower?'

'I hadn't thought of that, but yes, I expect so.'

'Christ,' said Patrick.

'Considering where we are, that's an appropriate comment,' said Lancelot.

'What happened next?'

'We had tea. We had it in Louise's sitting room. Scones and jam. Marigold poured. Brian proudly said that she'd made the scones, explaining that Marigold had been so fond of Louise at school, and was delighted to help out at a sad time in her own life. She looked so smug, Patrick. She's a dreadful woman. I would have taken against her even if I hadn't seen what I did.' And Louise had looked frightened. Her eyes had sought his in a way that broke his heart; on earlier visits, as her condition deteriorated, she had sometimes seemed bewildered, but not scared.

'Under the circumstances, it would be understandable, however regrettable, if Brian had a mistress tucked away somewhere,' said Patrick. 'But not there, not in their house. Like Lady Macbeth,' he added.

'But it was in their house – the Macbeths,' said Lancelot.

'You're not thinking she – or they – killed Louise, are you?' Was this why Lancelot had wanted to see him so urgently?

'No. At least, I don't think so,' said Lancelot. 'Louise caught a cold and it developed into pneumonia. She had a nasty cough the day I was there. She died at home, but by then there were proper carers looking after her. Amy insisted and Hugh supported her. I rang her straight away and said that Marigold seemed to be a thoroughly unpleasant woman and not fit to be near Louise. They had a showdown with their father and made him send her packing.'

'Did you tell Amy what you'd seen?'

'I couldn't. But she knew. They paraded it, touching one another, even in front of me. Marigold left, weeping, saying Brian needed her, Amy said.'

'But what now? I'm so sorry, Lance, it's a dreadful tale, but it's over, isn't it?'

'No. Either Marigold has stolen, or Brian has given her, two rings, some pearls, various other brooches and things and a small Boudin painting. I noticed it was missing when I went there that day. It hung on the wall near Louise's chair. There was a calendar hanging in its place.'

'A Boudin?'

'Yes. A lovely little seascape. She'd inherited it from an aunt. Brian said Louise probably lost the bits of jewellery. Said she'd got so vague she might have thrown them away with the rubbish. But she wouldn't have thrown the Boudin away. Amy says she doesn't care about the bits and pieces but she's afraid Marigold has designs on more. On Brian, in fact. She might marry him. She came back to the house, to help to sort out Louise's things, she said. Luckily, Hugh sent her off again, saying her presence was inappropriate. She left, with Brian promising her that they'd go out to the house in Provence as soon as things were settled. He said this in front of Hugh and Amy.'

'Oh dear,' said Patrick. 'But suppose Brian gave her these things, aren't they hers to keep? Legally, if not morally.'

'Certainly not,' said Lancelot. 'And Amy said he seemed surprised that they'd gone, but he covered it up. Said maybe one of the carers had taken them, but that wasn't possible. They were above suspicion.'

'Hm. The value of the jewellery would be obvious, but the Boudin? Would she have known about that, if she's as ignorant as you imply?'

'Maybe not just how valuable. But it was small and easily hidden.'

'So what do you want to do?'

'Get them back and expose Marigold as a liar and a thief.'

'I see,' said Patrick. 'Where do we start?'

'Here,' said Lancelot. 'In Marlow. She lives here.'

As the two men walked away from the church, Lancelot told Patrick that Amy had tried to find out about Marigold's past. She and Hugh had feared that the woman might intend to come to the funeral, but she had stayed away. Brian had commented on it, regretting her absence.

He'd gone mad, of course, Amy had said. The father she had loved and admired had not been equal to the demands of her mother's illness, and he could not be wholly blamed for that; many people in his position would have faltered, but his conduct had been indefensible.

'Amy did some checking,' Lancelot said. 'After that visit, when I met the woman, I suggested she should see if any of Louise's contemporaries could remember Marigold at school, but she'd married – her name would have been different. Amy knew some of her mother's old friends, and several came to the funeral. No one could remember a Marigold, but people sometimes use their second names or change them. Amy even looked out some old photographs – the tennis team, school groups, that sort of thing – but there was no one in the least like her in any. People do change, though. Age alters faces.'

'Did anyone look on Brian's computer to see if he'd been logging on to datelines?' asked Patrick.

'Hugh did, while Brian was away for a night. He had been surfing around all sort of things,' said Lancelot.

'Where did he go that night?' asked Patrick.

'Who knows? They think he was with Marigold.'

'If Brian really wants to marry her, I don't see how they can stop him,' said Patrick. 'People do these things, and there's the rebound factor to consider.'

'My idea is that perhaps we can discover something about her past that will convince even Brian that she's a schemer who's set her sights on him. When they got together with their computer dating, or however they met, she must have thought her ship had come in.'

And the danger of the intrigue, its squalor, could have been part of the appeal to Brian. Patrick knew this; he would explain it to Lancelot later.

'Have you a plan?' he asked.

'I thought we might call. Or you might. She knows me,' said Lancelot. 'You could pretend to be looking for a neighbour – make some excuse. You're good at that sort of thing.' Patrick's curiosity had led to his becoming involved in various episodes in which murders had been solved.

'She'll be out,' he said.

'Maybe. But you could ask about her. Enquire next door, that sort of thing,' said Lancelot.

'Do we know where Brian is today?' asked Patrick.

'Yes. That's why we've got to act now. He's in Edinburgh at a charity committee meeting. He's the chairman. And I've got the registration number of his car, in case he turns up suddenly. It's a Mercedes,' said Lancelot.

'Hmph.' Patrick, who liked cars, had a Saab, comfortable and functional but not exciting. He had left it in a large car park near the river. Lancelot also had left his Peugeot there. 'Let's have some lunch and think about this,' he said.

Over steak and kidney pie in a pub near the river, they talked about other things. Lancelot was writing a book about nautical explorers – Christopher Columbus, Vasco da Gama, Raleigh, Cook – examining their characters as well as describing their expeditions. Patrick had recently published a book about cross-dressing in Shakespeare; it had been well, if modestly, received.

After they had eaten, there was no avoiding it any longer; they had to find the house where, Amy had assured Lancelot, Marigold lived. Hugh, furious with his father, and mortified, had found the address on Brian's computer, printing off a map, muttering about employing a private detective.

The house was in a small close not far from the river. It was one of a row of attractive cottage-style houses, built in pairs, with small gardens and parking spaces in front.

'I'll wait here. You walk past,' said Lancelot. He looked nervous, pulling up the collar of his coat in a manner which advertised, 'Look at me, I'm up to no good.'

'I think you'd better go away,' said Patrick. 'Go back to the church and wait for me there.'

'What if they close the church?' said Lancelot.

'If all else fails, we'll meet at the Compleat Angler,' said Patrick. 'But the church is nearer. Here,' and he pulled a substantial paperback volume from a poacher's pocket inside his jacket. 'That'll keep you quiet for a bit.' It was a collection of short stories by several award-winning crime writers.

Lancelot took it. He had never known Patrick not to have some volume within easy reach, often about his person.

'You have such a fixation on skulduggery,' he complained. 'Reading this stuff.'

'If I hadn't, you wouldn't have asked for my help now,' Patrick said. 'And Shakespeare wrote some pretty good crime stories, don't forget.'

Lancelot went off chuckling, which cheered Patrick as they parted. Then, aware that Marigold's address was number seven, he walked down the road and rang the bell at number two. As he went up the short path to the front door, he could see through the window a narrow strip of garden with some shrubs and a shed at the end. There was no reply, so he moved next door. Here, a small gnarled stone gnome – not a gaudy one but a tasteful, venerable creature, peered at him from beneath a lavender bush near the front step. Patrick made a face at it and rang the bell.

An elderly woman came to the door. She opened it on the chain and looked suspiciously at Patrick. She's been advised not to open the door to strange callers, he thought; despite my respectable appearance I might be a thief.

'I'm so sorry to disturb you,' he said. 'I'm looking for Mrs Marigold Berowne, but I'm afraid I can't remember what number her house is.'

'It's not this one,' said the woman.

'Do you know which it might be?' It was the sort of quiet area where neighbours were likely to be on nodding terms, at least, with one another.

'No,' said the woman. She still held the door on the

chain, but her manner was more relaxed and she smiled at him. 'It's not next door. They're the Fosters – they're both out – and next to them are the Davenports, a very nice retired couple. They might know, I suppose. They've been here longer than I have.'

You're so careful with your door, but you've already told me more than you should to a stranger, thought Patrick. He had learned, in a long life, that when he cared to use them, he had winning ways, though they had not always won him what he most desired.

'I'll try them,' he said. 'Mrs . . .?'

'Mossop,' she said.

What a nice man, thought Mrs Mossop, closing her door, so tall and good-looking with that floppy grey hair. She had almost offered him a cup of coffee, but you couldn't be too careful these days.

Patrick reflected that it would be easy to become a conman. And Marigold was probably a conwoman who had trapped Brian at his most vulnerable.

He walked straight round to the Davenports. They had a trellis, trained with roses, crossing their garden. There were no visible gnomes.

Mr Davenport came to the door. This was probably an area which drew the retired, or the newly widowed, Patrick decided, estimating Mr Davenport's age as about seventy. He was small and rotund, with a pleasant face, almost a gnome himself.

'Mrs Mossop thought you might be able to help me,' he said. 'I'm looking for Mrs Marigold Berowne and I'm sure this is the right road, but I don't seem to have her number.'

'Ah!' Mr Davenport's door was not on the chain, but he was peering cautiously round it. Now he opened it wider. He looked thoughtful.

'Well, now,' he said. 'There are no Berownes in the

close. I know that, because I run the Neighbourhood Watch in this area.' Then he frowned. 'There's a house-sitter at seven,' he said. 'Tall, red-haired woman. I don't know her name and she's been out when I've called. Doesn't do much sitting, if you ask me. She's been away quite a bit this past month or two.' He regarded Patrick now in a less friendly manner.

He doesn't care for Marigold, thought Patrick.

'I don't actually know her,' he said. 'But as I was coming to Marlow, a friend asked me to look her up. Said he'd known her a few years ago and lost touch.'

It wasn't much of a story, but it worked.

'Merry widow, if you ask me,' said Mr Davenport. 'She has a few callers when she's here.'

'Men friends?' Patrick tried to look worldly.

Mr Davenport nodded.

'Bit worrying, really, but it's her business, I suppose. I was more anxious about her being away so much. The Tarrants are in South Africa visiting their family and touring around. They'll be away for another two months.'

'Is she there now?'

'Yes. Got a new car – she had a clapped-out old Ford,' said Mr Davenport. A spanking new Honda Civic was parked outside number seven. A present from Brian?

'Well, I'll go round, then,' said Patrick. 'Thanks.'

He walked slowly past number six, glancing across to look through the window. In the garden, he could see a large raw concrete object in the centre of a lawn. It was too big to be a bird bath; it must be a fountain, but how stark it looked. He remembered his sister Jane applying yoghurt to age a stone cupid she had bought to adorn an alcove in her garden. Patrick wasn't sure about the cupid but Jane had said it would blend in nicely when it had mellowed. All these houses seemed to have long front rooms. Patrick turned into the short entrance to number seven, where the silver-grey Honda Civic was parked.

This was a squalid business. A man much his own age, suffering the distress of a beloved wife's mental collapse, had given way to – what? Baser instincts? Grief? Simple need? He had met this Marigold under false pretences; Lancelot was confident that Amy's research could be relied on. And now Lance expected Patrick somehow to trap her.

There was no sign of movement in the house as Patrick pressed the front door bell and heard it chime, but she came to the door promptly. She was ugly. That part of the description was accurate, but she smiled at him in welcome. She wore a green knitted dress and a lot of make-up.

'Mrs Tarrant?' he said, smiling back, disliking her instantly before she had spoken a word.

'Who wants her?' she asked.

Patrick gave his true name.

'I'm a former colleague of her husband's, but I've never met her,' he said. He was about to invent a reason for calling but changed his mind; on the principle of setting a thief to catch one, a confidence trickster might be good at spotting another.

'And I'm a friend of them both,' said Marigold. 'I'm staying here while they're away.'

'Oh?'

'They're in South Africa. I'd had to give up my home after my husband died, and they offered me sanctuary here,' she said.

She was certainly plausible.

'I'm sorry – I mean, about your loss,' said Patrick. What a good thing Lancelot wasn't standing here beside him during this performance. 'But how fortunate that the Tarrants could help.'

'Yes, and it helps them too. It's not always wise to leave a house empty for long,' she replied.

While this went on, Marigold had summoned a tear to her eye and she dabbed at it with a tattered tissue, at the same time giving Patrick a shrewd, assessing glance.

'Of course,' he agreed. Then, as if he had been selling doubleglazing door-to-door for years, distinguished academic Patrick Grant moved slightly forward, adding, 'I am sorry to have upset you.'

'Oh dear, silly me.' Marigold dabbed at her eyes again, stepping back.

She's a bit of a mug, thought Patrick, or is she a sucker for any man? Though his big coat had a poacher's pocket within its folds, he wore a tie, dark corduroy trousers, and his shoes shone; he must look reassuring. Or even a prospect?

He was in. She had retreated further into the hall and he closed the door, mumbling something about the draught.

'Can I get you some water?' he said. Somehow they had moved into the sitting-room while Marigold still looked tearful. This was how she got Brian, he thought, perhaps reinforced by sexual wiles I don't want to think about.

'Oh, would you? Through there—' Marigold waved a hand in the direction of the kitchen. 'There's a glass somewhere about.' She sank down on to the large sofa.

There was a cut-glass tumbler on the drainer, and there was a wine glass containing dregs; there were also a plate, knife and fork, and a used mug. Marigold had not washed up her lunch, nor, possibly, her breakfast. Patrick ran water at the sink, rinsing the tumbler and filling it, and while the tap ran, he wrapped the fork in tissues from a box on the window ledge, slipping it into his useful big pocket. Then he filled the electric kettle and switched it on.

'Here you are,' he said, offering her the glass, and added, 'I've put the kettle on. I thought you might like some coffee or tea.'

Marigold had dried her fake tears and was leaning back on the big sofa.

'That would be lovely,' she said.

Patrick bustled back into the kitchen; he clattered about looking for cups and saucers or more mugs, and, seeing a dishwasher beside the sink, put the dirty things in it. That would mask his theft. As the kettle boiled, she entered the kitchen.

'You've tidied,' she said. 'How kind.'

'Not at all,' said Patrick. He had found a tray and now carried it back into the sitting-room, urging Marigold to precede him. She resumed her seat on the sofa as he set it down on a low table in front of her. Patrick did not dare sit beside her. He chose a chair on the far side of the room.

Marigold reached out for her coffee and took a quick glance at her watch. She's expecting someone, he thought. Brian? Back from the airport after his Scottish trip?

He drank his coffee, talking about Marlow, the river, the two churches. She listened and nodded. Then he rose.

'I must go – I'm taking up your time,' he said.

'Well, I am expecting someone,' she answered. 'A solicitor – business, you know. My husband's estate. Affairs to settle. So good of him to come here.'

'Yes. Well, I hope things sort themselves out,' said Patrick, who could not bring himself to wish her well.

'Time heals,' she said, as she led him to the door.

Patrick went straight back to the gnome-like Mr Davenport, who came promptly to the door when he rang.

'May I come in?' Patrick said, without preamble, and he

was past the small man in seconds. 'You're the Neighbourhood Watch official here?'

'Yes.'

'Do you have connections with the police? They know you?'

'Yes.' Mr Davenport beamed. 'Yes, I do. The co-ordinator, and also Inspector Lovesey. I know him from the Rotary.'

'You seemed a little concerned about the Tarrants' house-sitter. Could you get on to the inspector? Could you tell him about your suspicions – the men callers – and ask if he could do a fingerprint check?' Patrick patted his pocket. There'd be DNA, too, on the fork. 'Say theft is suspected.'

Mr Davenport's bushy white eyebrows shot up but he wasted no time. While he talked to the inspector, Patrick saw a car drive past; it stopped outside number seven and a man wearing a raincoat and a trilby hat got out. After Marigold had let her visitor in, Patrick stepped into the road to note the car's registration number. It was a blue BMW.

'Luckily Lovesey was there. We're to go round now,' said Mr Davenport.

'May we collect someone on the way?' Patrick asked. 'At St Peter's Church?' If Lancelot wasn't there, they could ring him at the Compleat Angler from the police station and get him to come over. He would lend gravitas to what Patrick would tell the inspector.

Mr Davenport hadn't had such an exciting day since he was caught in a blizzard in Cumbria several years before and had to spend the night in emergency accommodation. He recognised Lancelot straight away when he emerged from the church with Patrick.

The inspector took their story seriously. Lancelot

mentioned the painting and the rings; Mr Davenport weighed in with the gentlemen callers. When Patrick produced the fork, Lovesey took it away. He soon returned.

'We'll go round there,' he said. 'She can refuse us entry but that in itself would be suspicious. I can get a warrant if necessary.'

Patrick and Lancelot, in Mr Davenport's Rover 25, followed Lovesey and a sergeant who went in an unmarked car.

'What, no sirens?' murmured Lancelot.

The BMW was still outside number seven. Lovesey rang the bell and knocked on the door, and the sergeant went round to the rear of the house. He was in time to catch the BMW's driver as he hurriedly left through the back door, still pulling on his raincoat. From Mr Davenport's car, the others saw number seven's front door open at last and Lovesey entered the house. Time passed. Patrick and Lancelot waited on Mr Davenport's doorstep. They saw the man in the BMW drive away; soon after that the sergeant came along and asked Lancelot to go with him to number seven.

'The inspector says you can identify a painting,' he said.

It no longer mattered that Marigold would recognise him; she would also know her nemesis. Lancelot went with the sergeant.

Patrick remained at number five with Mr Davenport. While they waited, Mrs Davenport, who had been at a flower-arranging demonstration, returned. Mr Davenport kissed her warmly, took her coat and said he would put the kettle on. They were clearly devoted. He told her that Patrick was there on a Neighbourhood Watch matter.

'I'll explain later,' he said, as his wife excused herself and went upstairs.

They were all sitting round the kitchen table with cups

of tea, eating chocolate cake, when Lancelot returned. He looked tired, asking if he might use the Davenports' cloak-room. When he joined them in the kitchen, however, he was more cheerful.

'They've taken her away,' he said. 'And her computer. She had a laptop upstairs. What a beautiful cake,' he added, accepting the large slice which Mrs Davenport had put on a plate before him. Then he turned to Patrick. 'She had a record,' he continued. 'Soliciting, and blackmail. Theft, too. They found a lot of stuff upstairs. More than she'd taken from Louise. The painting was safe. Amy can have it now.'

He would tell Patrick the rest later. The prints on the fork had identified her; her real name was Gladys Brown. Lovesey was unlikely to need Patrick as a witness as there were plenty more prints in the house and on other items that were probably stolen.

'I think I'd better get in touch with the Tarrants,' Mr Davenport said. 'They'll have to know.'

'How did they come to employ her?' asked Patrick.

'She advertised on the Net, and in some magazines,' said Lancelot. 'The police haven't finished checking up on her. They think she made a habit of preying on elderly men and blackmailing them. She overstepped the mark when she went after Brian.'

They refused Mr Davenport's offer of a lift back to get their cars, and as soon as they left the house, Lancelot rang Amy on his cell phone. Patrick did not own one.

'I wonder what Brian will do,' said Patrick.

'He won't apologise. He might say he was taken in at a time when he was under great stress, but I doubt it,' said Lancelot. 'It will all be dusted away and never mentioned again.'

He was probably right. They walked on in silence. Then Patrick spoke.

'We'll have got tickets for overstaying our time in the car park,' he said.

They had.

TOUPEE FOR A BALD TYRE

A Misadventure from the Motor Trade Years of Harry Barnett

Robert Goddard

Swindon, 24 September 1970

If he had stayed in the pub, even for another five minutes, it probably would have been all right. Rillington had more or less said as much, which only made the thought more tantalising. Another five minutes; another pint; another gently blurred afternoon: for once, they would have added up to prudent business practice. Instead, Harry had returned dutifully, if far from soberly, to Barnchase Motors at half past two that afternoon – and found a visitor waiting for him.

'I was just about to give up on you, Mr Barnett,' Rillington explained, smiling thinly.

Harry sensed it was the only kind of smile that ever crossed his face. Rillington was a lean, sombre, narrow-eyed man of sixty or so, grey-suited, grey-haired, grey-*skinned*. On the early-morning train journey to work that Harry imagined him taking, he would attract no one's attention, draw no one's glance, challenge no one's preconceptions. Yet here, seated stiffly on the other side of Harry's desk, briefcase clasped flatly in his lap, pursed lips emphasising his trimmed moustache, he did pose some kind of challenge. That much was already certain.

'Your secretary didn't seem to think it was worth my while waiting.'

'No?' Harry caught Jackie's eye through the glass partition between his office and the outer room where she fitted occasional typing and telephone-answering into her nail-filing regime. Her devotedly plucked eyebrows arched meaningfully. 'She must have misunderstood. With my partner away for the day—'

'That would be Mr Chipchase.'

'Yes. He, er . . .'

'Is cheering on a horse at Newbury even as we speak, I dare say.'

'Ah, you—'

'Your secretary mentioned he was . . . entertaining some clients at the races.'

Clients? If only, Harry thought. But all he said was, 'Quite,' grinning manfully and shooting a glare at Jackie, who by chance or contrivance was no longer looking in his direction. His gaze reverted glumly to Rillington's card, which lay before him on the blotter, forming a small oblong of orderly typography in a jungle of scrawled telephone numbers, jotted mark-up calculations and obscene doodles.

C.E. Rillington
Motor Repairs Standards Assessor
H.M. Ministry of Transport
St Christopher House
LONDON SE1
Tel: 01–928–7999

'So what can I . . . do for you, Mr Rillington?'

'I'd like you to clarify a few points for me, Mr Barnett.'

'Oh yes?' Harry lit a cigarette, hoping he would appear what the advertisements for the brand promised – as cool as a mountain stream – but gravely doubting it. 'Smoke?' He proffered the pack to Rillington.

'I prefer a pipe.'

'Well . . .'

'Shall we get on, Mr Barnett? I'm sure we're both busy people.'

'Right.' Harry took a spluttering draw on the cigarette. 'Of course.'

'I popped into your workshop while I was waiting.'

'You did?'

'Young fellow called Vince showed me around.'

'Excellent.' I'll strangle Vince with a fan-belt, thought Harry. Slowly. 'Helpful lad.'

'Indeed. Not that he could help me with the . . . statistics of your operation.'

'No?'

'Your province, I rather think. Yours and . . . Mr Chipchase's.'

'Statistics, Mr Rillington? I'm not . . .'

'They can be the very devil, I find. But they tell a story. There's been a push to apply them to my field in particular since this government came into office. Computers are the future, Mr Barnett. We're only nibbling at the edges of what they can achieve.'

'Really? I don't know much about that kind of—'

'Take the Korek, for example. Feed its findings to a computer and—'

'The what?'

'The Korek, Mr Barnett. Not heard of it?'

'Dr Who's latest enemy?'

'Very amusing.' Rillington looked anything *but* amused. 'It's a machine that pulls out crushed car bodies, using air-operated rams to reverse the effects of a crash. We can then check the manufacturer's dimensions against the final size and shape.'

'Amazing.'

'And revealing. If the car fails to reach those dimensions, it's generally because it never did. Now, why might that be, do you suppose?'

'Can't imagine.'

'You're aware of the disreputable practice of welding together the intact halves of two damaged cars to produce what looks, to the hapless buyer's eye, like a pristine ready-to-drive-away bargain?'

'Well, I . . .'

'The Korek finds that trick out every time.'

'Does it?' Harry distractedly tapped ash off his cigarette and locked eyes hopelessly with Monsieur Michelin, who beamed up at him from his perch on the rim of the ashtray. 'How very clever of it.'

'Now, taken together with a separate investigation of tyre blow-outs where the driver, if he or she is lucky enough to emerge in one piece, reports recently fitting remoulds which, upon inspection—'

'What have remoulds got to do with body welding?'

'At first glance, nothing, Mr Barnett. But therein lies the beauty of the computer. It correlates the statistics, you see. It crunches the numbers and spits out . . . overlaps.'

'Overlaps?'

'Common sources . . . of cars that fail the Korek test . . . and tyres that have been remoulded a couple of times too many. At *least* a couple of times.'

'I see.' Dimly and queasily, Harry did indeed begin to see. The blind eye he had long turned to Chipchase's profitable innovations on the repair front had suddenly descried a disturbing vision.

'Bad luck? Bad workmanship? Or something more sinister? That's what we're bound to ask ourselves when the statistics point us so compellingly to a particular garage.'

'Well, I . . .' Harry puffed out his cheeks. 'I suppose you would be.'

'Vince and his less talkative colleague . . . Joe is it?'

'That's right.'

'They both seemed competent enough to me. Capable, even. Well capable.'

'Oh . . . good.'

'And I don't believe in luck.'

'You don't?'

'Which brings us—'

'Here's that tea I promised you, Mr Rillington,' trilled Jackie, as she toed the door abruptly open and entered with a tray bearing two cups and saucers and a plate of digestive biscuits. 'And coffee for you, Mr Barnett.' *Mr Barnett?* Jackie was evidently on her best behaviour, a small mercy for which Harry could not summon much gratitude. 'Black, I reckoned. Was that right?'

'Spot on,' mumbled Harry, noticing as Jackie plonked the tray down on the desk that Rillington's gaze left him and slid appreciatively up Jackie's long and shapely legs to the hem of her miniskirt, which at that moment Harry judged could scarcely be concealing very much. The man was evidently not immune to temptation. A chink in his armour, perhaps? But a small chink, in evidently thick armour.

Jackie minced out. Rillington's eyes swung back to Harry. 'Sugar?' Harry ventured.

'No thank you.'

'Biscuit?'

'Just the tea, I think.' Rillington took a sip.

'Righto.' A gulp of strong black coffee cleared the last of the beery fug from Harry's brain. But clarity did not furnish inspiration. 'So, where, er . . . were we?'

'How long have you and Mr Chipchase been in business together, Mr Barnett?'

'It's, er . . . five years now.'

'Did you take this place over from someone else?'

'Knight's Motorcycles. They, er . . . went bust.'

'And how long had *they* been in business?'

'Oh, seven or eight years. Until the late fifties there were fields here. The Belmont Brewery used to graze their dray-horses—' Harry broke off, smiling awkwardly. 'I'm sure you don't want a local history lesson.'

Rillington turned and squinted out through the window into the serried ranks of Barnchase Motors' used cars, gleaming in the sunshine on the forecourt laid where Harry had once as a child fed carrot-tops to Belmont's magnificent beasts of burden. 'Sounds like a veritable lost Eden,' Rillington murmured.

'I wouldn't go that far.'

'And we can't turn back the clock anyway, can we, Mr Barnett?'

''Fraid not.'

'Good Lord.' Rillington's squint honed itself into a concentrated peer. 'Is that an E-Type you have out there?'

'Yes. I, er . . . believe it is.' A midnight-blue 1962 Jaguar E-Type 3.8, to be precise. A snip at four hundred and ninety-nine guineas. A snip, indeed, at whatever price Rillington might be willing to pay. 'Fancy a test drive?' Harry asked impulsively.

'I wouldn't mind . . . taking a look.' A tinge of pleasurable anticipation had crossed Rillington's face. He sipped his tea, but his eyes remained fixed on the shimmering come-hither bonnet of the E-Type. Here was a second chink in his armour, one Harry was far better placed to exploit than the fleshy allurement of Jackie Fleetwood. 'I wouldn't mind at all.'

No more than a few minutes later, the two men were seated side by side in the car, Rillington's hands sliding slowly round the steering-wheel while Harry jingled the ignition key against the Jaguar's-head fob in what he judged to be a tempting tintinnabulation.

'Nought to sixty in seven seconds,' he purred. 'Top speed of a hundred and fifty. Really blows the cobwebs away.'

'I'm sure,' said Rillington.

'I could do a very special deal . . . for someone in your position.'

'No doubt.'

'What do you normally drive, Mr Rillington?'

'A Hillman Imp.'

'Well . . . need I say more?'

'Probably not.'

'Why don't you take her for a spin?'

'It's an idea.' Rillington smiled, less thinly than before, and moved his left hand from the steering-wheel towards the dangled ignition key. 'But not as good as *my* idea.' His hand froze.

'Sorry?'

'Once my report on this place hits the appropriate desk, you'll be for the high jump, Harry.' *Harry?* 'You and your racegoing chum, Barry. It could be a police matter. It could be . . . the end of the line.'

Harry swallowed hard. 'Surely . . . not.'

'Oh yes.'

'But . . .'

'Cut as many corners as you have here and, sooner or later, you're bound to come to grief.'

'But . . .'

'Fortunately for you, there's a way out.'

'There is?'

'And it doesn't involve me taking this overpowered heap of junk off your hands.'

'No?'

'No. It involves something more . . . *recherché*. Which isn't French for remould.'

'I, er . . . don't . . .'

'Need to say a thing. Just listen. While I tell you a little story.' Rillington leant back in his seat. 'I used to do a bit of cycling, you know. Took it seriously. CTC membership. Fifty miles every weekend. Eighty every other. Proper racing bike. No half measures. Then, one Sunday morning, the bike let me down. The gears seized solid. There wasn't a thing I could do with it. I hadn't got far, so I wheeled it home, planning to strip it down in the garage. I got back several hours before I was due, of course. Bit of a surprise for the wife. More of one for me, though. I caught her with the husband of one of her Townswomen's Guild friends. In a compromising position, you might say. Very compromising. In fact, so compromising I'd never even thought of it. An eye-opener. Yes. You could certainly call it that. Now, why am I telling you this pitiful tale of the cuckolded suburbanite?' Good question, Harry thought. 'Well, you may be surprised to learn that Mrs Rillington and I are still together. It was a simple choice, really. I preferred trying to satisfy her exotic tastes to indulging my hurt pride and turning into a bitter and lonely old man. To tell the truth, I *enjoyed* trying to satisfy her tastes. And, if I say so myself, I succeeded beyond her expectations. She no longer needs to look elsewhere. Oh my word no. But continued success requires continuous innovation. Mrs Rillington has recently expressed an interest in unusual locations for lovemaking. Bearing in mind her enthusiasm for all things rubber, I think I may have found the ideal venue. Your workshop, Harry. Plenty of tyres, most of them bald enough to avoid tread marks, adaptable to any required height or juxtaposition. And plenty of authentic, grease-smeared, petroleum-scented atmosphere. I can see it now. I almost feel it now. As for Mrs Rillington . . .' Rillington released a long, slow, anticipatory breath. 'Enough said, I rather think.'

'You want to . . . use our workshop to . . .'

'It's her birthday tomorrow, Harry. We're making a long weekend of it. Starting tonight.'

'*Tonight?*'

'Why not?'

'Well, I . . .'

'Barnchase Motors can get a tick in every box from me. *If* you help me out. But if you're going to go all prissy on me . . .'

Harry smiled nervously. 'There's no question of that. I mean, in this line of business, the customer is always right.'

'Glad to hear it. So . . .' Rillington flicked the still suspended ignition key with his forefinger. 'I don't think that's the right key. Do you?'

'Didn't think you'd get rid of him so easily,' said Jackie when Harry returned to the office after giving Rillington his key to the side-door of the workshop. 'I told Barry he had bad news written all over him.'

'Barry?'

'He phoned while you were out on the forecourt. Wanted to make sure everything was going smoothly, apparently.'

'I trust you told him it was.'

'Not exactly, no. Well, I didn't think it was, did I?'

'So, will Barry be rushing back to bale me out?'

'Didn't get that impression. Anyway, you don't need baling out now, do you?'

'No. As a matter of fact, I don't.'

'How *did* you get rid of him, then?'

'Who?' Harry countered coyly.

'Rillington. The guy with the wig.'

'Wig?'

'That hair's never natural. Didn't you notice?'

'Can't say I did.'

'Creepy, I'd call him. Could be a bit of a pervert on the quiet.'

'You reckon?'

'With that wig? And those X-ray eyes of his? Definitely kinky, I'd say.'

'Would you?' Harry yawned, exhaustion pouncing on him now the crisis was past. He could feel a doze coming on. 'Would you really?'

Harry was the last to leave Barnchase Motors that afternoon. Chipchase had not returned, which would have been unsurprising in the normal course of events but was utterly predictable given what Jackie had told him. MoT officials were not his company of choice. He was probably skulking in a pub in Newbury, fearing the worst. The thought gave Harry some small amount of pleasure. He would have to have a serious word with him about what Joe and Vince had been getting up to at his instigation. Harry would have to put his foot down. Firmly.

But that could wait. There was an evening of gentle recuperation to be passed first. A pint at the Beehive; collection of dirty washing from his house; delivery thereof to his dear and doting mother, followed by consumption of one of her steak and kidney puddings; several more pints at the Glue Pot, and an earlyish night. Just the therapy his frayed nerves needed. As for what might be happening in the workshop back at Barnchase Motors while he was thus engaged, he could only imagine. With relief as well as incredulity.

Chipchase finally put in an appearance as Harry was nearing the end of his first pint at the Glue Pot, entering the bar with his coat collar turned up and the brim of his racing felt angled over his eyes as if he was intent on being taken for a fugitive.

'Hellfire, Harry,' he said as he sat down. 'Am I pleased to see you.'

'Worried about me, were you, Barry?'

'You bet.'

'But not enough to hurry back and face the music with me?'

'Well, pulling the wool over some nitpicking bureaucrat's eyes is more your speciality than mine. I didn't want to cramp your style.'

'That a fact?'

'And you look chipper enough, so I'm guessing you got said bureaucrat off our backs.'

'You guess right.'

'How'd you manage that?'

'All in good time, Barry. Let's begin with *why* he was on our backs in the first place.'

Chipchase's response to Harry's account of Rillington's visit to Barnchase Motors was a characteristic blend of bombast and blandishment: Harry had never wanted to know exactly how the profits he shared in had been generated and it was too late to start now, even supposing there was any substance to Rillington's accusations, which naturally there was not; but Harry's negotiation of a solution to the problem qualified as a redeeming masterstroke.

'Wouldn't mind being a fly on the workshop wall tonight, hey? You played a blinder there, Harry old cock, you really did.'

'I'm glad you think so.' Harry was finding censoriousness difficult to maintain as pint followed pint and lurid images filled his mind.

'Got a mental picture of Mrs Rillington, have you?'

'Big woman, I should think.'

'Yeah. With a bit of a spare tyre.'

Harry finally cracked at that and descended into tearful mirth. 'Several spare tyres tonight,' he managed to say.

'In all kinds of juxtapositions,' Barry hooted.

'Oh dear, oh dear.' Harry dried his eyes as best he could. 'I wonder if his toupee'll stay on.'

'I doubt it.'

'Did you say toupee?'

They did not at first appreciate that the question had come from a third party. Eventually, however, as the gale of their laughter blew itself out, they noticed a man staring at them round the corner of the settle. He was a small, shrunken, whey-faced fellow of indeterminate age, dressed in a threadbare ratcatcher's coat and a greasy pork-pie hat.

Without waiting for an answer, he slid round, Mackeson in hand, and joined them at their table. 'Sounds like you could be talking about a mate of mine.'

'I doubt it,' said Harry.

'Fred Christie. Streaky, hawk-eyed bloke with a 'tache but not a strand of hair north of his eyebrows to call his own.'

'Never met him.'

'Are you sure about that? Only—'

'What does your mate do for a living?' put in Chipchase.

'How d'you mean?'

'Simple question, old cock. What's his line of work?'

'Well . . .'

'And what's yours, while we're about it?'

'Look . . .' The man leant forward and lowered his voice. 'I need to find Fred. Pronto. If you know where he is, I could, er, make it worth your while to point me in the right direction.'

'But Harry's already told you. We've never met him.'

'He, er, could be using a false name.'

'Oh yeah? Why might that be?'

'Let's just say . . . there are reasons.'

'Then we'd best be hearing what they are.'

'They're, er, private. Between him and me.'

'Not any more they aren't.' Chipchase gave the man a less than genial wink. 'Not if you want to get a chance to talk them over with Fred.'

'Are you saying you know where he is?'

'I'm saying we'll come clean if you'll come clean.'

The man squinted at each of them in turn. He did not look persuaded of the case for soul-baring.

'Have a think about it,' Chipchase continued. 'Harry and I are just off. We'll wait in my car. It's the Wolseley parked over the road. Two minutes.' He raised a pair of fingers. 'Then we skedaddle. So . . . don't think about it too long.'

'What are you playing at, Barry?' Harry demanded as soon as they were outside.

'Following my nose, Harry. Always a good policy.'

'You can't seriously think that creep really is a friend of Rillington's.'

'The description matched, didn't it?'

'That's rich. I was the one who met Rillington, not you.'

'Thin. Moustache. Toupee. You telling me that isn't Rillington?'

'I'm telling you—'

Chipchase whipped the driver's door open and flung himself in, slamming it behind him. Harry sighed heavily, opened the passenger door and clambered in.

'I'm telling you,' Harry resumed in a level tone, 'that there isn't a single good reason to believe a word this bloke says.'

'No?'

'Of course not.'

'How about your MoT man's choice of moniker?'

'What?'

'According to our friend, his real name's Christie.'

'So?'

'Like the murderer.'

'Like the actress too. And the whodunnit writer. I don't see—'

'Never mind them. Where did Christie the *murderer* live, Harry? Tell me that. Surely you remember. It was all over the papers.'

Enlightenment dawned slowly on Harry in the Swindonian night. Christie the murderer. Of course. Harry had even flicked through a book about the case his mother had borrowed from the library. He really should have remembered the title. His pseudo-civil-servant visitor of earlier in the day clearly had. 'Ten Rillington Place,' he murmured.

'Exactly.'

'Bloody hell.'

'Looks like you've been had, Harry. And here comes the man who can tell us why.' A shadowy figure in a pork-pie hat had just emerged from the Glue Pot. He peered suspiciously about him, then headed towards them. 'Leave this to me.'

As the man slid into the seat behind him, Harry sensed all was not quite right.

Long before he could have said why, however, he felt something cold and hard pressing into the back of his neck.

'Yes, Harry, it's a gun,' said Fred Christie, aka C.E. Rillington of the Ministry of Transport. 'One false move by you or Barry and your brains will be all over that windscreen.'

'Bloody hell.'

'Exactly. Very bloody indeed.'

'Calm down, mate,' said Chipchase, characteristically recommending a course of action he was obviously not following himself. 'There's no—'

'I'm not your mate, Barry. And I'm perfectly calm, thank you. But I *am* a little short of time and patience, so we'll dispense with the niceties. I tried the roundabout route and it didn't work. How much did Arnie tell you?'

'You mean the owner of that hat?'

'The very same.'

'Well, nothing really, except he knew you . . . and . . .'

'You weren't from the MoT,' Harry finished off, swallowing hard. 'We, er, stepped out here for a word in private.'

'And that's what we're having, Harry. Arnie's collecting his thoughts in the Gents. He'll be collecting them for quite a while, actually, so there's no immediate rush, but we do need to press on. Once I'd checked the workshop, I realised we'd have to resume our conversation on a more realistic basis. I asked after you at the pub where you take your liquid lunch and they mentioned several other watering holes where I might find you. This was second on the list. I imagine Arnie came here because it's close to the station. He'd have been hoping to get some directions. Geography's not his strong point. Never was.'

'You and he . . . go back a long way, do you?'

'Too long. But let's get to the point. Where's my money?'

'Money?'

'Don't act dumb with me. I kept a careful mental note of the burial spot. It was a tricky exercise, pacing out across your yard and workshop what I originally paced out across a field. But there's not a shadow of a doubt. I checked and double-checked. The inspection pit is exactly where I buried the money – and several feet deeper than I dug. Well,

Arnie did most of the digging, to tell the truth, but that doesn't give him any prior claim in my judgement, considering I went down for a longer stretch and we'd have been caught in possession but for me thinking on my feet. Now, you said Knight's Motorcycles owned the site before you, didn't you, Harry?'

'Yes,' came a hoarse response in what Harry barely recognised as his own voice.

'Did they have an inspection pit?'

'No.'

'So, you installed it?'

'Yes.'

'In that case, I return to my original question: where's my money?'

'We don't know,' said Chipchase.

'You dug the pit. Harry's just admitted it. You couldn't have avoided finding the money.'

'*We* didn't dig it. We got a builder in.'

'Sharland,' said Harry, his heart sinking as he realised the significance of the builder's identity.

Now it was Chipchase's turn to say, 'Bloody hell.'

'What about Sharland?' snapped Christie.

'Our workshop was the last job he ever did,' Chipchase replied. 'He had a big Pools win straight after and retired.'

'A Pools win?'

'So he said.'

'And where did he retire to?'

'Spain, wasn't it, Harry?'

'Florida, I heard.'

'*Shut up*.' The pressure against Harry's neck increased. 'Why should I believe any of this?'

'Well, there's the fact that Sharland's bronzing himself in some palatial villa in the sun . . .' Chipchase began.

'While we're still stuck here in Swindon,' Harry rounded off.

'Bit of a choker for all of us,' Chipchase went on. 'No wonder the last time I saw the bloke he was grinning like the cat that's got the cream. Not that I know how much cream there was, of course.'

Christie said nothing. Harry's heart was thumping in his ears. A rivulet of sweat was inching down his temple. His breaths came fast and shallow.

'What now?' Chipchase asked eventually.

'Now?' Christie responded, as if from some more distant place than the rear seat of the car. 'You'd better start driving.'

'Where to?'

'Head west. Towards the motorway.'

'There's not a lot more we can—'

'Just drive.'

'Okay, okay.'

The bleak thought formed in Harry's mind that this was likely to be a one-way journey. Either Christie believed them, in which case he was probably planning to kill them before going after Sharland. Or he did not believe them, in which case . . .

'That's funny.' Chipchase had got no response from the starter. He turned the ignition key off, then back on and tried the starter again. To no effect. 'The engine's dead.'

'Don't play games with me,' said Christie. 'Start the bloody car.'

'I can't.' There was another futile wrestle with ignition key and starter. 'It's dead as a doornail.'

'Do you take me for a fool? *Get this thing moving.*'

'I can't, I tell you.'

'Barry,' Harry put in, 'for God's sake—'

'I'm not kidding, Harry. It's kaput.'

'But you've just driven it from Newbury.'

'I know, I know. It doesn't make sense.' Chipchase glanced back at Christie. 'Why don't I take a look under the bonnet? There must be a loose connection.'

'There'd need to be a loose connection under *my* bonnet to fall for that one.'

'It's God's honest truth. I don't know what's the matter with the thing. Let me give it the once-over. You'll still have Harry as hostage. I'm not going to leg it with an old mate's life on the line, am I?'

Harry closed his eyes for a second, praying silently that Chipchase might for once be relied upon.

'All right,' said Christie after a long and breathless moment's thought. 'Go ahead.' He pushed his door open. 'But remember: I'll have time to plug you as well as Harry if you try to scarper.'

'Okay. Understood.' Chipchase climbed out, moved round to the front of the car and raised the bonnet, obscuring their view of him.

'*Stand where I can see you,*' shouted Christie.

Chipchase edged back into view round the nearside wing. He secured the bonnet-strut, then peered down into the engine.

'*Now you know how it feels.*'

The voice had carried distinctly through the still night air, though where it had carried *from* Harry could not have said. His eyes swivelled in search of the source.

'That Zephyr you sold me conked out the second trip I took in it.' The source materialised in Harry's field of vision, striding towards Chipchase along the pavement. 'And what did that mealy-mouthed partner of yours say? Not our problem. Well, it is *now*.' It was Mr Gifford, outraged and out-of-pocket buyer of one of Barnchase Motors' less durable used cars. Harry recalled a recent conversation with him. It had not ended harmoniously. 'Since I can't drive my car, I don't see why you should be able to drive yours, *Mr* Chipchase.'

Chipchase seemed lost for words. He glanced up at the approaching figure of Gifford – a bullet-headed, square-shouldered fellow carrying some weight he looked intent on throwing around – then gaped helplessly back at Harry through the windscreen.

'There's *Mr* Barnett as well,' roared Gifford, pointing an accusing finger at Harry. 'Get yourself out here and join the fun, why don't you?'

'Bloody hell,' murmured Harry.

'Come on.' Gifford yanked Harry's door open. 'Let's be having you.'

'Bugger it,' said Christie. Quietly and decisively.

Harry flinched at the words and closed his eyes, reckoning the odds were heavily weighted in favour of Christie pulling the trigger at that moment.

But he did not pull the trigger.

The pressure was suddenly removed from Harry's neck. There was a scuffling sound behind him. Then a pounding of running feet on paving stones. He opened his eyes. Both Chipchase and Gifford were looking past the car along the street. Harry turned to look in the same direction.

Just in time to see the pork-pie-hatted, toupee-sporting figure of Fred Christie vanishing at a trot round the corner into Faringdon Road.

'Who's that?' demanded Gifford.

'You don't want to know,' Chipchase replied, leaning back against the wing of the Wolseley and tipping up the brim of his hat to wipe the sweat off his brow. 'Believe me.'

'I thought . . . he was going to shoot me,' Harry said unevenly. He made to climb out of the car, but his legs buckled beneath him. Gifford had to help him out in the end, frowning in puzzlement at his sudden conversion from saboteur to saviour.

'What's going on?' Gifford asked, almost solicitously.

'Long story,' said Harry.

'He dropped the gun,' said Chipchase, pointing to a dark shape lying a few feet away in the gutter. 'Can you believe it? He dropped it and ran.'

'Gun?' Gifford stared at them in astonishment. 'You mean there are customers of yours even more pissed off than me?'

'In a sense,' mumbled Harry.

'But a *gun*? That's a bit strong.' Gifford stepped towards the discarded weapon, then stopped – and laughed.

'What's so funny?' growled Chipchase.

'This gun.' Gifford stooped and picked it up.

'Be careful with it.'

'Don't worry. It's not connected.'

'Connected?'

'It's a petrol-pump nozzle.' Gifford held it up for them to see. And a petrol-pump nozzle was indeed what they beheld. 'Gallon of thin air for you two?'

'Bloody hell,' said Harry.

'He must have filched it from the workshop,' said Chipchase.

'Let's hope that's all he filched.'

'Where's he gone?'

The shout had come from the doorway of the Glue Pot. They turned to see Arnie, bare-headed and even wobblier on his feet than Harry, staring blearily across at them and rubbing what was presumably a tender spot behind his left ear.

'That way,' said Harry and Barry in unison, pointing in the direction Christie had taken off in.

'He won't give me the slip this time,' Arnie declared optimistically before setting off in tepid pursuit.

A brief silence, born of general disbelief, fell upon them. Then Chipchase said, 'Maybe we should phone the police.'

'Never thought I'd hear those words coming out of your mouth, Barry,' Harry responded, truthfully enough.

'Neither did I.' Chipchase shrugged. 'Anyway, I only said *maybe*.'

'What about my car?' Gifford cut in, seeming suddenly to remember his grievance.

'What about *mine*?' Chipchase countered.

'Listen.' Harry's spirits had revived sufficiently for him to assume the role of conciliator. 'Come to the office tomorrow, Mr Gifford, and I'll give you a full refund for the Zephyr, plus ten per cent for the inconvenience you've been put to.'

'If you think you can fob me off with a rubber cheque, you've got—'

'Cash in hand. And call it quits. Provided you replace whatever vital part you took out of this Wolseley, of course.'

'Well . . .' Gifford softened. 'I suppose . . . that'd be all right.'

'Hold up, Harry,' said Chipchase under his breath. 'I know you've just had a nasty experience, but don't you think you're getting a bit carried away? A *full refund?*'

'In the circumstances, I reckon we can afford to be generous.'

'Yeah? Well, there's generous and there's over-generous and then there's plain bloody crazy. We don't have to—'

'Tell you what, Barry. You can stay out here and haggle with Mr Gifford if you like. Or you can join me in the pub. But I need a drink. And it won't wait.'

So saying, Harry turned and steered a straightish path across the street towards the Glue Pot, tossing back a concluding comment over his shoulder as he went.

'It's up to you.'

THE HOLIDAY

Clare Francis

Melanie Briggs decided to lay out her clothes two weeks before the holiday: not so soon that time would begin to drag, but not so late that she couldn't enjoy the sight of her new dresses to the full. She wanted to make the most of the build-up, not simply because the holiday would mark the end of the worst year of her life, but because the preparations, the small tasks and rituals, were about the only thing that got her through the day. Already she had the cruise brochure propped up beside the kettle so she could leaf through it while she ate her breakfast, and for an hour or so every evening she sat, with the cat curled in her lap, poring over the itinerary. The mornings were still bad, though, and she hoped that the sight of her beautiful new dresses would ease the moment of waking with its lurch of memory, and give her courage to face the day.

She had lived in the small basement flat at 27 Albany Road for fifteen years. Every Saturday morning she did the weekly shop and cleaning. During her troubles she'd bought lots of sweet doughy food and let the cleaning slide, but on the day she was to lay out her clothes she shopped for slimming products and cleaned the flat from top to bottom, washing the net curtains and bleaching the slime off the area steps. By the time she'd finished, she felt a sense of achievement and rather wished she'd got around to it before.

Finally, after a coffee and a low-calorie cereal bar, she began on the clothes. From the shelves she gathered some of the old faithfuls that had taken her to the Costas in her twenties and early thirties: strappy sandals, T-shirts in the bright colours she loved, shorts and skirts – those that hadn't become too much of a struggle around the waist and hips at any rate. Then, in a concession to the advancing cellulite, she added two sarong-style wraps, one green, one red, to conceal her upper thighs on the walk back from the sun deck.

If these clothes seemed all too familiar, even dreary, the evening dresses she pulled out of the wardrobe more than made up for it. There were four of them, all brand new, all long and slinky, in bright satiny fabrics with glittery straps and embroidered tops. She'd hesitated over the red one because its low-cut back would necessitate going bra-less, not something she was too confident about, but when she'd phoned from the shop Debbie had brushed her doubts aside. 'Go for it, girl,' she'd cried. 'Don't give it a second thought. You've got great boobs! Sport 'em and flaunt 'em, I say!' And Melanie, in a surge of recklessness, had bought not only the dress but an expensive pair of matching shoes as well.

She hung the four evening dresses high on the wardrobe door and stood back to admire them. Even in the gloomy November light they shimmered and gleamed like jewels. Though she could never hope to compete with Debbie in the beauty department, with these outfits she could at least match her for style. And they had chosen a cruise where style was going to count. Thirteen nights on the QM2, New York to the Caribbean and back.

Originally they'd thought of going on a package to St

Lucia, but most of the resorts there seemed to be geared to couples or families, while the rest didn't offer much in the way of social fixtures, and both women agreed they wanted somewhere with a bit of life to it – Debbie because she was naturally sociable, Melanie because she'd always feared missing out. Brought up in a neat semi, the only child of quiet, home-loving parents, she'd felt from a young age that life would always pass her by, a suspicion that had deepened in adolescence and been reinforced ever since. But with Debbie there was no danger of missing out, and for once in her life Melanie could look forward to being in the thick of things.

Fanning out the skirt of the red dress, seeing the way it caught the light, Melanie had the overwhelming urge to tell Debbie how wonderful it looked. During the week, unless Debbie was especially busy in her hairdressing salon, they usually spoke mid-morning, Debbie chattering about the laughs they'd have on holiday and the people they'd meet and the champagne they'd drink 'morning, noon and bloody night' while Melanie laughed, and fought back tears of gratitude because she couldn't believe how lucky she was to have such a friend, someone who had not only scooped her up and set her back on her feet when she was at her lowest ebb, but now, astonishingly, was coming on holiday with her.

But it was Saturday morning, the salon's busiest time. Melanie phoned a little nervously, and wasn't surprised to wait a good two minutes before Debbie came on the line.

'Sorry,' Melanie said immediately. 'Is it a bad time?'

'It's a madhouse,' Debbie declared with satisfaction.

'I'll call back later, shall I?'

'No!' Debbie exclaimed, with a snap of her lighter and an audible intake of smoke. 'Let 'em wait. I've been dying for a cig.'

'It's just that I've just been laying out my clothes.'

There was a puzzled pause. 'Laying out? As in *flat*?'

'Putting them where I can see them.' In case Debbie should think this a bit odd, Melanie added quickly, 'To make sure I haven't forgotten anything.'

'Oh, *right*! Bloody hell, Mel, wish I was half as organised as you. But you know me – I'll be up till two the night before, chucking things in and out of suitcases. Packing for England.' Debbie gave her distinctive throaty chuckle. 'Never have been able to get my act together.'

'It's two weeks tomorrow. I can hardly believe it.'

'Well, it can't come a moment too bloody soon, that's for sure!' Debbie liked nothing better than to complain about her business and her clients, both of which she adored.

'I can't believe it's really happening.' Melanie's voice caught with emotion.

''Course it's happening! And you and me are going to be the belles of the ball.'

'The red dress – it's so lovely, Debbie.'

'Just wait till you make your grand entrance. They won't know what's hit 'em.'

'Oh, Debbie . . .'

'Now, don't get all wobbly on me,' Debbie said kindly.

'No, no . . . I'm just so happy to be going, that's all.'

'You and me both.'

'Really?'

'*Really.*'

'Even when you could have gone with anyone?'

'Well, I'm not going with *anyone*, am I? I'm going with *you*.'

'Yes, but—'

'Oops,' Debbie cried suddenly. 'Got to rush. My next lady's getting restless. Bye, now, darling. You take care, eh?'

'Yes.'

'Now, you'll call me if you start to get wobbly, won't you?'

'Yes.'

'Promise?'

'Promise.'

'Good girl,' she sang. 'And, Mel . . .?'

'Yes.'

'That dress is going to knock 'em dead!'

She laughed as she rang off, and Melanie felt a fresh wave of relief. However often Debbie might reassure her, Melanie could never shake off the worry that her new friend would have second thoughts about the holiday and wish she was going with one of her more outgoing girl-friends, not to mention one of the two men she was currently stepping out with. Debbie said she wanted a rest from men, that they were too much like hard work, but Melanie couldn't believe she really meant it. Debbie had been married twice, admittedly, and was never short of admirers, but to reject all men on principle seemed unwise. Melanie could only hope that, after all the support Debbie had given her, she didn't find the holiday a disappointment.

Melanie's terrible year had started with her fortieth birthday, which she'd been quietly dreading for some time. To be single at thirty was a disappointment, but at forty it was an admission of failure. People began to think there must be something wrong with you, and deep in her heart Melanie suspected they were right. She'd been married once, in her early twenties, to a cabinetmaker called Darren who'd upped and left after less than a year, saying he couldn't stick marriage after all. She thought she'd never get over the shock, but at that age you can get over almost anything and within six months she'd persuaded herself that she was well rid of him. As the years passed, though, she'd begun to look back on the loss of Darren with something like regret. She wondered if he hadn't been her best bet after all, that with more effort she might have kept him, though quite what form this effort might have taken she couldn't think, since she'd been the one to do all the shopping and cooking, cleaning and ironing, saving and budgeting.

After Darren, love had never seemed to come her way. There'd been occasional drink-fuelled episodes with men she could barely bring herself to look at the next morning. There'd been men who'd made it clear they wanted to keep it at friendship. And there'd been a couple of relationships she'd had hopes for which had fizzled out for no apparent reason. She began to wonder if she put men off in some way, but when she went back over everything she'd said, the gestures she'd made, the expressions she'd used, she could never work out what it might be. She wasn't especially pretty, of course, and she'd put on a bit of weight over the years, but you only had to see the wives of some of the men at work to realise that plain looks were no barrier to getting a good man. And it wasn't as if she didn't make the most of herself, dressing neatly in the bright colours that suited her best, having her hair cut by Debbie, and going up to London for her clothes. Once, a man had remarked on how well groomed she was, a compliment she had treasured over the years and done her best to live up to. But grooming clearly wasn't enough, and after all this time she was beginning to wonder if she'd ever find out what was.

Debbie suggested she might be setting her sights too high, but if you didn't aim for love, what was the point? And it wasn't as if Melanie didn't know what love meant. Ever since childhood, she'd enjoyed a vivid inner world, which, as she grew older, intensified into a rich, all-enveloping dream-life, an exquisite universe of beauty and success, misunderstandings and reconciliations, love and rapture. Most of the time she loved dream-men, singers or film stars or TV celebrities, but then, out of the blue, it would be someone at the insurance company where she worked, a handsome man glimpsed in the canteen or through the glass partition of a meeting room, or the manager of the bowling alley where she went on Thursday evenings, or a cousin's brother-in-law, and then she would experience long months of sweet, agonised longing, heightened by distant sightings of the loved one, even the exchange of a few treasured words. When her dream-life was at its best, it became so intense that she would often experience a kind of euphoria, like the rush of a drug, that lifted her free of the real world into a state of ecstasy.

She knew what it was to experience the ultimate; if it hadn't yet come her way in real life, she was prepared to wait.

In her dreams, though, she never reached forty. It sent a shiver down her spine, the first hint of the long winter ahead.

Two months after her birthday, she went as usual to her mum's for Sunday lunch. Her dad had died when she was eighteen and she'd stayed close to her mum ever since, living at home till she met Darren, persuading him they should take a place in the next street, then, when he left, finding the basement flat in Albany Road so she could drop in on her mum three or four times a week. But on this Sunday Melanie arrived to find the curtains drawn, the back door locked, and her mum lying cold and dead on the bathroom floor. She must have screamed because a neighbour appeared. Then there were ambulance men and people she didn't know, and a doctor she'd never met before who treated her for shock.

A pulmonary embolism, they told her the next day; death would have been almost instantaneous. The *almost* rang and rang in Melanie's brain. She saw her mum lying alone and helpless on the cold floor, her life slipping away and no one to hold her hand. She saw her crying out for help and berated herself for not phoning the evening before, for not going round earlier, for not realising that something was wrong. Her mum had died alone, and she would never, ever forgive herself for it.

People handed her forms and asked for documents. They told her she must register the death, but the place where she had to go was miles away and she couldn't face it. Instead, she sat helplessly in her mum's kitchen, drinking warm Chardonnay and shuffling papers through a fog of tears. A couple of words swam into focus. *Post mortem.* Hastily she pushed the paper away, she didn't want to read things like that; yet the more she tried to blot out images of her mum's body lying exposed on a slab, of unspeakable humiliations being visited on it, the more graphic these images became, and then it got so bad she couldn't eat or sleep, and when she did finally sleep it was so deeply she could barely wake up again.

Eventually her cousin Dave arrived and took over the arrangements. Neighbours called round to offer their condolences or pushed notes through the letterbox before hurrying away. Melanie's boss phoned to say she must take as much time off as necessary, and her colleagues in the accounts office sent a large wreath. But once the funeral was over and her cousin Dave had gone back to Ealing, everything went quiet again. No one came round, except to leave a cake on the doorstep, which Melanie ate in the course of a single afternoon. In the end, she took her mum's cat back to the flat in Albany Road and drew the curtains and unplugged the phone and switched off her mobile and went to sleep. She slept all day. The doorbell rang a couple of times, but she didn't answer. Then, it must have been a day later, there was a loud hammering on the door which kept on and on without stopping. It was her cousin Dave, saying she was ill and really had to go and see a doctor.

She didn't think she was ill, but she was too tired to argue. When they got to the surgery the receptionist said her old GP had left and she would have to see someone new. But she didn't want to see anyone new, she wanted to go straight back to the flat, but her cousin calmed her and wouldn't let her leave, while the receptionist assured her that the new doctor was really very nice.

As soon as Melanie entered the consulting room she realised the receptionist had tricked her. The new doctor wasn't nice at all, he was large and bull-like and his tone when he asked her to sit down was brisk and unsympathetic. He ignored her while he tapped something into his computer, and when he finally turned to her his eyes were cold and hard. She began to cry, she couldn't help it, she buried her head in her hands and sobbed loudly. To her surprise she felt a light hand on her shoulder and heard a kind voice say he was very sorry about her mum and she was to cry as much as she wanted to. She must have poured out her heart for well over the allotted fifteen minutes, but he never tried to cut her short. He just listened and patted her shoulder from time to time, and told her that her mum wouldn't have suffered, that in the unlikely event that the embolism hadn't killed her instantly, then it would certainly have rendered her unconscious. He explained that post mortems were done with thoughtfulness and dignity, and told her very firmly that she mustn't think about it again. She might have stopped crying at that point, but he asked if she had anyone to look after her, if there was a friend or relative she might be able to stay with for a while, and then the grief and loneliness welled up again.

When her tears finally ran dry, he pressed some fresh tissues into her hand and said that regular crying and plenty of exercise and fresh air were worth a hundred anti-depressants, but he would still prescribe some if she wanted him to. He looked proud of her when she said she would try without. 'Good girl,' he said. 'Remember – plenty of long walks and fresh air. And cry whenever you feel like it.' He told her to pop in again the following week, sooner if she felt the need.

She went back four days later. The sign over his door said, Dr Geraint Davies. Now that she wasn't crying, she got a proper look at him and realised he was younger than she'd first thought, probably in his late thirties. She couldn't imagine how she'd ever thought him unsympathetic. Certainly his features were large and rugged, with heavy brows and a sportsman's broken nose, but his voice was just as kind as before, and he had an attractive way of tilting his head and looking at her a little sideways when he spoke, of telling wry jokes against himself and muttering conspiratorial asides she couldn't believe he made to anyone else. She felt she could trust him, and took his advice to heart. She cried as often as she felt like it and made herself walk to the shops and back, even dusted off her old bicycle and went for a ride around the park. When she saw him again the following week, she was able to tell him truthfully that she was feeling much better. He beamed at her. 'Good girl. I knew you'd do it. One more bit of advice – go out and enjoy yourself. Remember, laughter's good for you. It's just been scientifically proven that it boosts your immune system and cheers you up.' He added in that confidential tone of his, 'That's scientists for you – spend a fortune to tell us the obvious!' He grinned, sharing the absurdity of it with her, and she found herself smiling back, the first time she'd smiled since her mother died. 'I don't know whether I *can* enjoy myself,' she said uncertainly. 'Of course you can,' he insisted. 'It's what your mum would have wanted. Phone up a friend. Go to a film. Have a drink. I don't usually recommend drink in cases of bereavement, but' – he peered sideways at her in that comforting way of his – 'I think you're sensible enough not to get too carried away.'

Melanie tried to carry out his instructions, but it wasn't easy. Every evening she resolved to be sensible with the Chardonnay, only to get carried away to the tune of a whole bottle. And she much preferred to stay at home with a DVD than phone one of her two friends from work to suggest going to a film. She did persist with the exercise, though, because it made her feel better. And, imagining how she must have looked to the doctor, she tried to make an effort with her appearance. The obvious place to start was her hair, which had got long and straggly, and she booked herself in to Debbie's salon for a cut.

She dreaded sympathy, it upset her badly, but Debbie expressed hers so naturally, so warmly, that it didn't upset her at all. Though they'd always chatted amicably while Debbie did her hair, Melanie would never have dared consider Debbie a friend, not when she was so popular, yet the moment Melanie came into the salon, Debbie embraced her and whisked her off to the staff room at the back of the salon for a coffee and a cigarette, and listened sympathetically, with real understanding, even at one stage made her laugh a bit. Melanie felt so happy after this, and her hair looked so good, that somewhat to her surprise she embraced Debbie back, and they arranged to meet for an early evening drink two days later. Soon, the evening drinks became a regular weekly event. And one Sunday Debbie suggested they go clothes shopping together, persuading Melanie to buy two rather glamorous suits, though neither was quite suitable for the office.

Melanie began to realise how lucky she was to have found not just one new friend, but two. The other, of course, was the doctor, and when she saw him in the adjacent queue at Sainsbury's one Saturday she didn't hesitate to wheel her trolley over and say hello. Since he was off-duty she was careful not to talk about herself, keeping instead to the wet weather and the length of the checkout queues that day. She could tell that he appreciated her thoughtfulness, because, having looked a little startled when she first rushed up, he quickly relaxed and talked about the international rugby match that afternoon and how he reckoned the wet ground would suit Wales, and she guessed, with the pleasure that comes from gaining a sudden insight, that his broken nose had come from his own love of the game. He certainly had the physique for it, the height and the broad shoulders and the muscular arms, and she had a sudden vision of him in white shorts, pounding down the pitch.

'Do you play rugby yourself?' she asked.

'Used to at medical school. But I'm way past the serious stuff now. Too slow, too unfit. Too old!' he added with a grin. 'These days I just play the occasional seven-a-side with friends. Lots of running and wondering where the hell the ball's got to. But it keeps me out of trouble.'

'I don't think I've ever seen seven-a-side,' Melanie said, having watched very little rugby of any description.

'You haven't missed much. It's great to play but not much fun to watch.'

'Oh, but it sounds very exciting. Very.'

While she searched for something else to say she looked

down at his trolley and noticed it was fully laden, a whole week's load by the look of it. She wondered why he should be doing the shopping when he must surely have someone to look after him. But even as she thought this, it occurred to her with a small beat of excitement that he might be on his own like her, that they got on so well because he too knew what it was like to be lonely.

The next moment, she rejected this as a foolish hope. Men like him were never single. Men like him always had a beautiful wife with shining hair and perfect skin. A wife who was too lazy to shop maybe, or a career woman who was never around to do the chores, or a mother of young children who was too tired at the end of the week. But beautiful nonetheless, because the failings of beautiful women never counted against them.

She heard herself ask, 'Do you like cooking?'

He had been frowning impatiently in the direction of the checkout where, two customers up the line, the assistant was laboriously entering a credit-card number on to the keypad by hand. 'Sorry?'

'Are you a cook?'

'Not really, no. Just breakfasts. Bacon and eggs, that sort of thing. Otherwise I'm completely useless. The microwave's about my limit.'

'I always think food never tastes quite so good out of the microwave.'

'You're probably right, but – well – they're handy things, aren't they? When needs must.'

He gave a smile, but she spotted the strain at the corner of his mouth, and the rueful glint in his eye, both so faint that no one else would have noticed, and realised she had stumbled on to a painful subject. He was probably forced to cook when he came home at night, to throw a scrappy meal together because his wife was still at work or having a migraine or lounging in the bath. Picturing him standing helplessly in the middle of the kitchen, exhausted after a long day, Melanie's heart went out to him in a wave of tenderness.

She said, 'I don't suppose you have the time, either.'

'Sorry?'

'To cook.'

'Ha! No.' As if to emphasise the point he looked at his watch, then at the queue, and made a face of patience wearing thin.

'I cook an omelette when I'm in a hurry.'

'Oh?'

'A sort of Spanish omelette with potatoes and vegetables.'

'Ah.'

'It's very easy, particularly if you have leftover vegetables . . .'

But he had been distracted by a woman who was squeezing past his back with the clear intention of barging into the queue ahead of him.

Melanie was about to glare at her when the woman dropped something into the doctor's trolley and said in a terse voice, 'They've run out. This is all they have.'

Dr Davies picked up the item, a jar containing some sort of red sauce, and said, 'Well, it'll do, won't it?'

The woman didn't reply but stared coldly into the distance. She was tall and blonde and elegant in a bony sort of way, with a sharp nose and lips that were all the thinner for being pressed tightly together.

The doctor turned to the woman and began to speak to her in a low voice. The way he turned his back on Melanie was apologetic, embarrassed, but Melanie longed to reassure him that he wasn't to worry, that she completely understood why he had to do it. Indeed – and it came to her quite suddenly – she felt she would always understand everything about him.

As the woman listened to the doctor, her gaze flicked restlessly around the store, briefly alighting on Melanie, looking straight through her as if she was of no importance, moving rapidly on again.

Melanie craned her head so she could see the woman's left hand. There was no ring on the third finger. Just a girlfriend, then? Or a wife who chose not to wear a ring? Whatever the relationship, it was clearly far from happy. The woman made no attempt to hide her anger with the doctor, first pursing her thin lips, then flexing her nostrils until the skin went white, then crossing her arms and holding them tight against her stomach. When the queue moved forward, she made no effort to help the doctor unload the trolley but stood sullenly beside the till.

The doctor's profile was very grim as he bundled the shopping onto the belt. Melanie longed to reach out and offer words of comfort, but she knew the value of silence at such a time, and kept the message of support to her eyes, so that when he looked at her, as she knew he would, he would be able to read it there. It was simply a matter of waiting, of keeping the understanding in her eyes until he turned and saw it. But then a jar he'd thrown carelessly onto a pile of vegetables began to topple, and, seeing her opportunity, she leapt forward to retrieve it.

'Oh, thank you, Miss – er – *Briggs*.'

'Melanie.'

'Melanie.' He flung her a smile, so warm, so startling, that her heart seized high in her chest and she could only stare at him, her message of understanding quite lost.

She thought of him constantly after that. She thought of him in the evenings when she sat in her sitting room at Albany Road. She thought of him when she lay in bed at night, and first thing in the morning when she woke. She practised breathing his name. Geraint. She was fairly certain it was pronounced with a hard G, but she phoned the Welsh Office just to make sure. She tried to memorise every detail of his face, the way his mouth turned down slightly at the corners, the way his nose skewed to the left at the site of the break, the colour of his eyes, a clear dark brown, and the way they twinkled when he was amused. She played his voice over and over again in her mind, hearing the slight Welsh lilt, remembering with a small thrill of fear the coldness of his tone when they'd first met, and with a shiver of joy the warmth and playfulness of his voice once they'd got to know each other.

The more she thought about the smile he'd given her in the supermarket the more she realised it had been a signal, a message that he'd read her thoughts and appreciated – no, *welcomed* – them. The question was, how long should she wait before seeing him again?

In the end she left it four days. To enable them to meet naturally, without strain or difficulty, she made an appointment to see him at the surgery on the pretext of not being able to sleep. The delay was an exquisite agony. By the time she reached the surgery her pulse was racing and she felt so hot she had to go and splash her face with cold water. In the waiting room she rehearsed her words, her expression, her tone, but the moment her name was called, her mind went blank. Her hand trembled as she opened the consulting-room door. She worried that he might not live up to her images of him. But she needn't have worried: he was everything she'd remembered, and more. Her pulse was beating high in her head, she felt oddly weightless, it was all she could do to walk calmly to the chair and sit down.

He glanced up from his computer and said, 'Oh, hello,

Melanie. Won't be a moment.' As he tapped away at his notes she reminded herself that he couldn't afford to show her any special attention, that for her sake as much as his own he had to pretend that their relationship was strictly that of doctor and patient. He must be seen to keep his professional distance. But in a strange way it made the whole thing more wonderful. It added the thrill of the forbidden, the excitement of the unspoken.

'So what can I do for you, Melanie?'

As she told him about her sleeping problems she used her eyes to send a different, far more personal message. Though he nodded gravely and looked down at the floor a couple of times, she felt certain he had read her message and understood.

'Living on your nerves a bit, are you?' he asked.

'What?'

'You seem rather nervous today.'

'Do I?' She felt the heat come into her face and said shyly, 'Perhaps I am a bit.'

He began to scribble on his prescription pad. 'Well, try these sleeping pills. Three nights should be enough to settle you back into your sleeping pattern. In the meantime, do your best to relax.'

He raised his eyebrows at her, and she suddenly noticed how tired and careworn he looked. The girlfriend was obviously giving him a terrible time. That was the trouble with women who were used to having things their own way – they made so little effort. They didn't give men what they needed: love and tenderness and understanding. Melanie felt a rush of protectiveness. She longed to ask him what the trouble was so that he could pour his heart out to her, as she had poured her heart out to him. But she knew this was forbidden, and for the moment at least she must follow the rules.

She went home in a state of restless determination. It wasn't hard to find out where he lived. She simply went back to the surgery at the end of the day and followed him home. He drove quite fast and she almost lost him when he went over an amber light which, heart in mouth, she was forced to take at red.

He pulled into the driveway of a modern house on an executive estate and let himself in through the front door. The garden was unkempt and one of the curtains in the front room was only half drawn. Later, when some lights went on, she saw him pass in front of a flickering television. Eventually the girlfriend arrived. It was just as Melanie had thought – they were not getting on together. No sooner had they gone into the kitchen than a furious row broke out. Geraint strode back and forth like a caged animal, gesticulating helplessly, clutching a hand to his head, while the girl spat out a stream of invective. Even from where Melanie was standing in the shadow of the hedge, she could hear the shrillness in her voice.

Two weeks later, the girlfriend moved out, and Melanie made an appointment to see Geraint at the surgery.

'How's the sleeping, Melanie?'

'Much better, thank you.'

He was putting on a businesslike front, but she could tell that he was heartily relieved at having got rid of the girlfriend. It was obvious from his voice and his eyes, which, though sharp, were more at peace.

'Managing without the sleeping pills?' he asked.

'Yes. I only wake the odd time now.'

'Good. Good. So?' He was asking if there was anything else she wanted. She met his gaze and in that instant it seemed to her that they exchanged a look of perfect understanding.

'I've just finished with my boyfriend,' she said.

'Ah . . .' He nodded a lot, and she could see that he was looking at her in a new way. 'And, er . . . is that proving a problem?'

'Oh no, it's a relief. We weren't getting on together. I never realised how much of a relief it was until we finally broke up.'

He nodded again, more slowly this time.

'We had awful arguments. They upset me so much I think that's why I wasn't sleeping.'

He had stopped nodding now, and was simply watching her.

'Rows are so upsetting, aren't they?' she said. 'Far more than you ever realise at the time.'

He made a noncommittal gesture, but she could see that he was struck by the coincidence in their circumstances and the new bond it had formed between them.

Melanie gave him her best smile. 'Now I feel I can move on and start enjoying life again.'

He looked away and moved a paper an inch across his desk. 'You've had a very hard few months.'

'Yes. But it's going to be all right now.'

'Really? I'm glad,' he said in a voice that was suddenly rather hoarse. 'So, er . . .' He cleared his throat. 'Anything I can help with on the medical side?'

She felt the heat rise into her cheeks. She was trembling as she said, 'Not on the medical side, no.'

The look he gave her then was unlike anything he'd given her before, searching, puzzled, but full of hidden meaning. For a moment he seemed to be plucking up the courage to say more, only to think better of it and scramble to his feet to open the door. He didn't meet her gaze as she left, but that was all right, she understood why. He had realised that something extraordinary had happened, and he didn't quite know how to deal with it.

After that, she went round to his house three times a week to make sure he was all right. She went on Mondays, Wednesdays and Fridays. Once, she'd gone on a Saturday and followed him to the rugby field, but she was so far away from the pitch she couldn't work out what was happening, and afterwards he went straight off to the pub with his friends.

Debbie guessed immediately that something exciting had happened.

'You dark horse, you!' she exclaimed, after Melanie had admitted there was someone in her life. 'What's he like? Do tell!'

Melanie didn't say too much. Her love was too precious for that. But she let Debbie wheedle a few facts out of her, that he was a professional man, handsome and rugged, a sportsman.

'And single?'

Melanie nodded.

Debbie whistled. 'Well, go for it, girl!' Then she added in her kindest voice, 'But take it slow at the same time, if you know what I mean. Best to let him set the pace, eh?'

A month later, Melanie cut her hand quite badly chopping vegetables and went to the surgery for an emergency appointment. Taking one look at the blood, the receptionist tried to persuade her to go to the A&E at the hospital ten miles away, but Melanie said she'd be quite happy to wait.

Geraint looked startled when he saw her, but she smiled to reassure him that nothing had changed between them, and their secret was safe. He asked the nurse to come in and assist him as he stitched up the wound. Melanie examined his head as he bent over her hand, admiring the way his hair curled slightly at the hairline, spotting a tiny scar she hadn't seen before, just above one eyebrow. His fingers were very hot where they touched her hand, it was like an electric charge, and to put them both at ease she chatted lightly about the weather and the sports news, because she knew that was the sort of thing he enjoyed.

He didn't speak until he'd tied off the last stitch. Then, as he went to wash his hands he said, 'What sort of a car do you drive, Miss Briggs?'

The Miss Briggs was a blind of course, because the nurse was there.

'A Polo.'

'Blue?'

'Yes.'

He turned to face her as he dried his hands vigorously on a paper towel. 'Would I have seen it near my house, by any chance?'

Melanie felt a twinge of unease. 'Well . . . I'm not sure I know where you live, Doctor.'

'Oh, but I think you do, Miss Briggs.'

Melanie gave a laugh that came out oddly, like a gasp. Suddenly she felt rather unwell. 'I've got friends in the same road, of course. They might have mentioned that you live there too. In fact, I remember now . . . Yes, they said . . . Yes . . . that you lived there too.'

'And who would these friends be exactly?'

'Oh, they . . . Oh, I . . .' She clasped a hand to her forehead and sank back in her chair. 'Sorry, but I'm feeling a bit faint.'

The nurse put an arm round her shoulders, but Geraint stood in front of her and said in a cold voice, 'Miss Briggs, you really must stop all this nonsense and get a grip. No more hanging around my house. And I'm afraid I'm going to have to ask you to find yourself another doctor.'

She cried most of that evening. He hadn't meant to hurt her of course, she knew that. In fact he would have been horrified to see how much he'd upset her. But there was no need to belittle her in that way, no need to say such cruel things when all she'd ever wanted was to watch over him and make sure he was all right. She would forgive him, of course, because she loved him and she couldn't live without him, but it would take a little time.

She was still a bit tearful when she went to meet Debbie the next day.

Debbie took one look at her and whispered, 'Are you all right, love?'

Melanie shook her head. Without another word, Debbie bought her a large vodka and tonic.

'Man trouble?'

Melanie nodded.

'They're all the same. Drive you crazy, then drive you mad. What's he done?'

'He wants to break it off.'

'And you still love him?'

Melanie could only nod.

'Well, it hasn't been long, has it? So maybe it won't be so bad as you think.'

'It's been three months.'

'*Three months!* But . . . I had no idea. From what you said I thought . . .'

'I wasn't sure I loved him at the beginning. That's why I never bothered to tell you.'

Debbie gave a sympathetic sigh. 'Ahh. And now you *are* sure, he wants out. Oh, you poor old thing.' She put an arm round her. 'You've had a real basinful, haven't you?'

Melanie cried some more.

'Well, remember – you've still got your friends. And your friends are your friends because they never let you down.'

The restraining order was served on Melanie a month

later. She was ordered not to approach Dr Geraint Davies either directly or indirectly at any time, nor go within a hundred metres of his home or place of work.

It was a horrible piece of paper, and it made her cry again.

She told Debbie that her lover had written to say he didn't want her anywhere near his house.

'*What*?' Debbie exclaimed. 'That's a bit uncalled for, isn't it? Why would he want to go and do a thing like that, for Christ's sake?'

'I don't know. I suppose he's found someone new, and he doesn't want any reminders of me.'

'But why would you want to go near his house anyway? That's ridiculous. No, from what you say you're well rid of him. Good riddance to bad rubbish, I say.'

It was Debbie who kept her going over the next few weeks, insisting they meet for drinks, taking her clothes shopping, phoning almost every morning. And then, in that moment of inspiration, suggesting the holiday. 'It'll do you good,' Debbie declared. 'And God alone knows, us girls need all the fun we can get.'

Every morning, when Melanie snapped on her bedside light and saw the new dresses, she wished she'd hung them up a good week earlier. They glowed in the dark little bedroom like tropical flowers, and just looking at them was enough to make here feel she was halfway to the Caribbean. It was no longer a struggle to get up, and she often left for work a good ten minutes early.

Her stomach still tightened a little when she drove in through the office gates – news of the restraining order had circulated like wildfire – but she no longer cared if people whispered about her in the canteen or stared oddly at her in the corridors. And in recent days she'd managed to silence the people who greeted her with the curiosity that masqueraded as exaggerated concern by saying she didn't think they were looking at all well, and asking if they were absolutely sure they were all right.

Her job in the accounts department required little conscious effort. While one part of her mind checked the columns of figures, the other dreamt of the holiday. She pictured Debbie and herself in different locations around the ship, parading along the deck, attending cocktail parties and black-tie dinners, Debbie at the centre of things of course, but Melanie close behind, champagne in hand, the sun on her back. Debbie said the holiday would bring closure to Melanie's awful year, and for the first time Melanie was beginning to believe it might actually be possible.

At a quarter to eleven every morning Melanie went outside for a smoke. Ignoring the sniggers and glances of the office juniors in the next doorway, she got out her mobile and waited for Debbie's call. If the salon was busy it wasn't always possible for Debbie to call, of course, but then she'd phone after work, or at the latest the next day. But first one day went by without a call and then another. Always prone to anxiety, Melanie immediately began to worry that something had gone wrong. Debbie was going to cancel. With ten days to go, she had finally realised the holiday was a mistake. She had found something better to do, or someone better to do it with.

Melanie left a voice message on Debbie's mobile, then a text message. She called the salon and asked to speak to her, but they said she was busy, and when Melanie said she'd hang on, they told her Debbie really couldn't come to the phone but would call her straight back. When Debbie didn't call back, the fear clutched at Melanie's stomach, the figures on the printout she was meant to be checking became a blur, and, saying she had a headache, she left work early to drive to the salon.

Debbie wasn't there. The stylists said they didn't know where she was, but she wasn't expected back that day.

Melanie went home but couldn't settle. She left two more messages on Debbie's mobile before getting back into her car and driving the twenty minutes to Debbie's house. As she drew up outside, she saw Debbie's car parked on the garage apron.

Debbie opened the door with, 'Oh, hello, Mel.'

Her tone was subdued and Melanie had the sickening certainty that her worst fears were about to be confirmed.

'I was worried,' she said.

'Sorry I didn't call back.' Debbie led the way into the lounge and stood by the fireplace. 'But I didn't want to tell you over the phone.'

'Tell me what?'

'My dad's ill. They think he'll have to have an operation. I'm sorry, but I won't be able to come on holiday.'

Melanie stood staring at her.

Debbie added, 'I'm sorry, but there's no way round it.'

Melanie's mouth had gone dry, she couldn't speak.

'You can always go on your own, you know. There's bound to be lots of other singles on a cruise like that. There always are. You'll get to know them in no time flat. End up having a wonderful time.'

Go on my own? she wanted to scream. *But I don't want to go on my own!*

Debbie went on calmly, 'But if you decide you want to cancel, you can always claim on your insurance. Just like I'll be claiming on mine.'

Melanie jerked her head from side to side in misery and disbelief.

'I'm really sorry, but there it is.'

Melanie must have been holding her breath because the next moment she felt dizzy and the room began to sway. She thought Debbie would help her to a chair, but she didn't move, she just stood there watching her.

When Melanie finally managed to speak, the words came out in a series of gasps. 'What's – wrong – with – your dad?'

'They're not sure. It's going to be an exploratory operation.'

'But . . . can't it wait?'

'No, it can't wait,' said Debbie sharply. 'It might be serious.'

'Can't they do it before we go?'

'They might. But I'm certainly not going to leave my dad just after a major operation. No way!'

Melanie groped her way towards a chair and sat down. The unhappiness surged up into her throat, her face crumpled and she began to sob wildly, like a child.

'Please don't,' said Debbie, and her tone was very cool.

'But I can't go on my own!' Melanie cried. 'I can't!'

'Then cancel.'

'I don't *want* to cancel. I want to go with you – on – the cruise.'

'Look, you've just got to face facts.'

Melanie wailed, 'You never wanted to go with me! I knew you didn't! Not really!'

'That's not true. Of course I wanted to go with you.'

'You were just pretending!'

'I don't pretend.'

Melanie sobbed again, 'But I don't want to go on my own. I don't!'

There was a clinking sound and after a moment Debbie pushed a glass into Melanie's hand and encouraged her to drink. It was whisky and she took two gulps.

'Now, you've really got to calm down. These things happen. It's not the end of the world.'

But misery and dread pulled at Melanie's stomach. It wasn't just the holiday, it was the tone in Debbie's voice. 'You're glad not to be going!' she wept. 'You're glad!'

'Look, just pull yourself together, and we'll talk about it another time.'

Melanie cried bitterly, 'So you *are* glad! I *knew* you were! I *knew* it!'

'All right. If you really want to know, I *am* relieved. Because you've been keeping things from me that you shouldn't have. You've not been telling me the truth. And after everything I've tried to do for you, I think the truth isn't too much to ask.'

Melanie gripped her glass and tried to control her ragged breathing.

'Why didn't you tell me about the doctor? Why didn't you tell me it was all in your mind? I mean, we all get the hots for blokes, we all get to fancy people, but a *restraining order* – well, you should have told me. I felt such a fool not knowing. I felt such a fool saying I was going on holiday with you and having this bloke give me a seriously strange look. Talk about the last to know!'

Melanie downed the rest of the whisky and got unsteadily to her feet.

'I mean, you should have told me you had a problem, Mel, and then I could have helped you find the right help. Because that's what you need, you know – proper help. I mean, your mum's death was a shock, of course it was, but to go stalking this poor guy – well, you can't do that to people, Mel, you really can't. He still hasn't got over it, you know. He's still worried that you're going to be hiding in the bushes—'

Melanie stumbled blindly towards the front door.

'Mel, wait! Wait!'

Melanie wrenched at the latch and ran for her car. She drove in the direction of home, then away from it, and got lost in a strange area. All the time a voice was ringing in her head: *There's worse. There's worse.* Deep down she knew what this bad thing would be, but she didn't want to think about it too much yet. First, she wanted to be sure. It was terribly important to be sure.

Eventually she found her way home and took a bath and had a couple of glasses of Chardonnay. Then she went to the top shelf of her wardrobe and drew out her black tracksuit and black hat, and put them on. Then, choosing a roundabout route, she drove to a road three away from the one where Geraint lived. She parked in the dark area between streetlamps and, taking the pencil-beam torch from the door pocket, walked to Geraint's house, keeping close to the front hedges.

He was out, but it wasn't too cold. She didn't mind waiting. She had her favourite place, behind a laurel in the garden of the house next door. Normally she would dream while she waited, but no dreams came her way tonight, and she thought instead about the red dress she would never wear, and the oceans she would never see, and the warm sun she would never feel on her back.

It was midnight before Geraint got home. She heard his car and looking through the hedge saw that he was alone. He went quickly to bed.

She was in no hurry. She felt exceedingly calm. She returned the next evening, and this time there were lights on and voices. His and a woman's. All the curtains were drawn and a new blind had been fixed up in the kitchen where there had been none before. But the blind hung a good inch clear of the window and barely reached the edge of the pane, so she could see a small area by the kitchen door. But by the time the woman wandered into view it hardly mattered because Melanie had already identified the woman's voice. It was Debbie's.

Melanie cancelled the holiday. Because of the short notice she didn't qualify for a refund, and since she had no insurance, there was no way of reclaiming the money.

On the first night at sea the two of them had planned a quiet evening. But on the second, which was a Sunday, they had decided to go for a gala night: long dresses, best hair and make-up, the works. So it was on the Sunday that Melanie put on her red dress and stood in front of the bedroom mirror, drinking Chardonnay and swaying to the strains of Sinatra singing 'Strangers in the Night'. Once the Chardonnay was finished, she drank a third of a bottle of gin and the dregs of some cooking wine. Finally, she took the rest of the sleeping tablets that Geraint had prescribed, along with all the Panadol she could find and a packet of Nurofen. The moment she lay down, the miracle happened. Her dream-world came back to her in all its glory, more vivid than ever. It took her higher and higher, until she was floating among the stars. As she drifted in and out of sleep she wept and cried out in ecstasy because her life was so perfect and so beautiful. She had loved and been loved. What more could she ever ask?

She didn't want to wake; she fought it all the way. But they wouldn't let her rest. Their voices kept breaking in, calling her name, cajoling her to wake up. When she did eventually wake up, she longed to sleep again if only to escape the noise and the bright lights and the things the nurses kept doing to her. She had tubes down her throat and tubes in her arm, a throbbing headache and a terrible thirst, and no idea of how she would ever cope.

They kept her in hospital for two weeks because they

were worried about what the Panadol might have done to her liver. Then, having decided her liver was out of danger, they sent her to a psychiatric unit for observation. There, two doctors asked her a lot of questions, sometimes one at a time, sometimes together. Once, she made the mistake of trying to describe her dream-world, but seeing their intolerant young faces, she stopped and never mentioned it again.

When she got home, she had to report to a new doctor, a woman who kept telling her she must be sure to take her drugs. The drugs made her drowsy, though, and after a month she decided not to pick up another prescription. Instead, she took herself to the Lake District and stayed in a youth hostel and walked for miles and miles every day.

One morning, she got up while it was still dark and watched the soft, pink dawn break over the lake, and cried out with joy because she had never seen anything so beautiful, not even in her dreams.

She sold her mother's house and gave up the flat in Albany Road, and bought a tiny cottage on the edge of a wood, where she put out large quantities of nuts for the wild birds. After much thought, she decided to stay in her old job because she felt at home there, and continued to shop at Sainsbury's because she knew her way around the shelves. Later, when the time felt right, she began to go out a bit, to the bowling alley at first, then a couple of the quieter pubs, because she liked the people there.

One evening in late summer, sitting in a pub courtyard with some friends from work, she was distracted by a woman's voice that she recognised, raised high in exasperation. It was joined by a man's voice that she also knew, pitched low in anger. The two voices argued back and forth for some time, over what sounded like well-travelled ground, until the woman suddenly cried, 'You know what? I really can't be bothered any more. I just can't be bothered!' A chair scraped back, high heels clacked furiously away across the flagstones, then, after a pause, there was the sound of another chair and slower, heavier footsteps.

Melanie didn't look round. She just looked at her friends and lifted the cool wine to her lips, and felt the warmth of the sun on her back.

FOOL OF MYSELF

Reginald Hill

'And what will you tell him in this letter of yours?' asked my mother as she lay dying.

'Everything,' I said.

'Then, as usual, you will make a very great fool of yourself.'

Even in death she spoke with such certainty.

And she was nearly always right.

Not this time, Mother, I thought as I swung the wheel over. Not this time!

Then I saw the tractor coming round the bend.

And my last thought was, oh shit.

Perhaps Mother was going to be right after all!

Dear Detective Superintendent Dalziel,

You don't know me, but I know enough about you to know you're a man of independent mind, above fear or favour. That's what I want, someone to understand, someone to be my voice.

So who am I?

My name is William Appleby. I am, and will now remain forever, nineteen. I'm an only child, my father dying when I was barely a year old. His car skidded off the Greendale Pass road and plunged into the gorge. It was recorded as an accident, but lately I have begun to wonder if it might not have been his last independent act, his bid for freedom.

But I'm getting ahead of myself.

I suppose that a son brought up by his mother alone must run the risk of being a 'mummy's boy'. It's a title I didn't mind. True, Mother was fearsomely protective, but at the same time she inspired a natural admiration and respect, not just from me but from everyone in our small town, and Yorkshire people aren't easily fooled.

And yet, if you look closely, you could find she achieved her reputation at least in part by making unacceptable offers of help, such as proposing our pocket-handkerchief lawn as the site of the church fete or offering her wedding ring (which it would have taken amputation to remove from her finger) as prize in the restoration-appeal raffle. Instead of direct contributions to worthy causes, she would dangle before them the hope of generous legacies, though always with the rider, 'Of course, my boy's fragile health means I first have to make sure he is properly provided for.'

I reckon my 'fragile health' was a trump card that got her out of a lot of tight situations. In fact it didn't consist of more than a slight tendency to get over-excited in certain situations, easily controlled by some mildly sedative capsules. Physically I usually felt on top of the world.

Another area where reality blurred a little was our finances. It was generally accepted that Mother, while not perhaps 'stinking rich', was certainly 'not short of a bob or two'. If anyone was bold enough to make direct enquiry, she might reply, 'Well, there's the house . . .'

(worth over a quarter million in the current market) . . . 'and I have a little invested in the funds,' contriving to suggest by the archaism both sharp financial acumen and a broad portfolio. In one sense this was completely true. No one could live as comfortably as she did on a widow's pension without knowing how to manage money. As for the portfolio, it was certainly broad. Susceptible visitors were permitted to glimpse a selection of annual reports from top companies scattered across the dining-room table before Mother with many apologies tidied them up, and the big calendar in the kitchen was always boldly annotated with mementoes of shareholders' meetings.

These 'susceptible visitors' were invariably men. Mother was an attractive woman, and knew how to maximise her attractions by dress, make-up and demeanour. But, as I eventually realised, the prize she dangled before her admirers was not her person but her portfolio. Passionate romantics were of little interest to her. In fact, I believe my own devotion fed all her emotional needs. What she set out to attract was men with calculator hearts; men who would wine her and dine her and buy her reasonably expensive presents (exchangeable for cash refunds); men who would always err on the side of caution in their sexual demands for fear of scaring her off; above all, men who, if they became too demanding, could soon be sent running for cover by the simple disclosure of the real state of her finances.

Am I trying to paint her as a monster? Certainly not. She was a human being following the same imperative that drives us all – survival. We are not simply born into this world, we are shipwrecked on it. The survivors are those who make the right choices.

I think after Father's death, Mother got all her choices right.

Except one.

A wise man, or woman, never comes between a dog and its bone, or a young man and his mate.

Adolescence arrived. I changed in all the ways that boys change. My devotion to Mother kept me from the extreme forms of teenage rebellion, but it could not damp down the fire in the blood.

You, Mr Dalziel, I guess are a man of the world and will know what I'm talking about.

I discovered girls. You might have thought that being such a mummy's boy, I might have developed some kind of quasi-incestuous fixation on older women. Far from it. What I wanted were girls who were teenagers like me, girls who would laugh and drink and dance with me, and enjoy what naturally followed without regret or recrimination.

Perhaps my freedom from any Oedipal obsession was down to a growing intuition of what really made Mother tick, though it wasn't till later when I went to university that I really began to look at her objectively. As a schoolboy I was too busy for analysis. If there'd been an EU subsidy for sowing wild oats, I'd have been a rich man. I never had any problem with getting girlfriends and I found Mother surprisingly unconcerned by my success. The few who lasted long enough to visit our house often told me how lucky I was to have such a compliant parent and wished they could swap her for their mothers-from-hell. When I passed this on, she smiled and said, 'You enjoy yourself, son. Just remember two things. Don't get serious and don't get careless.'

But of course I did get serious. There was this girl

in the sixth form, Gina Lovegrove, daughter of Dan Lovegrove, the brewer. Three months after we started, we were still going out, and my friends were regarding us as an item.

Then suddenly we were done. No big scene. She started backing off, went clubbing with her mates, let some other guy take her home, that was that. I had one of my little bouts of mental over-activity which the capsules soon put right. Back to normal and determined to show I was cool, I soon took up with another girl, Kelly Hall, who was as blonde as Gina had been dark, and had left school to work in the family hotel business, so no overlap there. And very soon I couldn't recall what I'd seen in Gina.

Then Kelly was gone too. She broke a date and when I rang her, she said she was sorry but it wasn't working for her any more. My thoughts and my pulse went racing again, the capsules did their work, and very soon afterwards I had the welcome distraction of leaving school behind me and heading for university. I packed my bags and went off to find whatever solace this new experience could offer.

Now for the first time I began to see Mother differently. Hitherto I had accepted her on the same terms as everyone else, which is to say as an attractive widow of independent means, full of community spirit, universally admired for her charitable works, her compassion for the needy, and of course her devotion to her child. Okay, so she had men friends, but there was no hint of scandal, just an acceptance that she was engaged in the impossible task of seeking a man worthy to be my stepfather.

During my teens I did begin to get the message that we weren't perhaps as well off as people thought.

While I never wanted for anything essential, I got few of the little luxuries I yearned for, like a motorbike. One day, looking for evidence to support my argument that if we had money to burn, I might as well burn some of it through the exhaust of a Harley, I did a bit of snooping through her bank statements, but all I found were the day-to-day transactions of a woman making ends meet.

I salved my unease by concluding that all our money must be tied up in shares. But a little later when I got accepted at Mid-Yorkshire Uni, which seemed quite perfect for me – only forty miles away, far enough for independence, close enough for easy access to home cooking, laundry and cash top-ups – I was flabbergasted to hear Mother wondering whether it might not make economic sense for me to commute from home!

'You mean we can't afford it?' I demanded. She backed down instantly, said there was no problem, no need to get myself excited. And that was the end of the matter.

But it stayed in my mind, and once I got to university and opportunities to run up bills came crowding, I decided I had to know just how well off we really were. Alone in the house during the Christmas vacation, I went looking for the statements from her shareholdings. What I found came as a real shock. They were worth a couple of thousand in total, no more. What was more, the house was mortgaged up to the hilt.

One other thing the search turned up was a scrapbook full of cuttings about you, Mr Dalziel. Mother was a real fan. I read through it, fascinated, and that's how I come to be sure you're the man to read this letter.

To confront her about her finances seemed impossible. I loved her too much to be her accuser. But I needed to work out what my new knowledge could mean.

I had all the necessary data, of course. A child sees far more than a parent realises. And gradually over the remainder of that vacation, as I matched memory with observation and analysis, I began to re-evaluate what I knew.

My conclusion was that the rumours of our wealth, the reputation for charitable open-handedness, the company AGMs and the share prospectuses, all were nothing but window dressing. Instead of taking one of the other routes open to a single mother – Social Security; menial work; remarriage; writing a bestselling novel! – she invited a certain type of man to subsidise our living style. Morally questionable? Perhaps. But she sold them nothing but their own greedy dream.

Of course it made me see her differently. I understood now just how ruthlessly single-minded she could be, but I felt just the same about her. Everything she'd done had been done for me.

So I resolved to watch my expenses for her sake, but no resolve could make me follow her advice about girls.

Once more I got serious. And this time I also got careless.

Michelle Powers was perfect for me. We shared so many interests and tastes it was unbelievable. She was gorgeous to look at and incredibly sexy. And she adored me as much as I adored her. I never met her family, who are reputed to own half of Mid-Yorkshire, but I didn't doubt I could win them round. As for mother, she and Mitch seemed to get on famously.

Once more I was on top of the world and this time I could see no reason why I should not remain there.

Then it happened again. This time much more dramatically.

Mitch vanished.

I hadn't seen her for a couple of days but we had a date on Saturday night. On Saturday morning, I got a text cancelling it, no reason given. Getting no reply to my return texts, I called at her flat. The girl she shared with, a media studies student called Donna who didn't much care for me, said she'd gone away for a few days. When I asked where, she answered, 'If Mitch had wanted you to know, I think she'd have told you,' and closed the door in my face.

I made enquiries among my friends. None of them could help, but one recollected seeing her a few days earlier, having lunch at a pub outside town with an older woman. From his description, I was certain it was Mother.

I decided to go and talk to Donna again.

I got on my bike (push-bike not a Harley, but a lot more use at the uni) and headed for the house where they had their flat. As I approached, I saw Donna unlocking her bike from the railings.

I pulled in behind a parked car and watched as she rode away. Wherever she was going it wasn't towards the media studies centre.

I followed.

Half an hour later, we were on the outskirts of town. Finally she turned into the drive of an imposing suburban mansion. A sign on the gate read, *The Cedars Clinic*.

I rode up the drive and left my bike beside hers outside the main door.

There were some rose bushes blooming on either side of the doorway. I picked a small posy and went inside. Donna had vanished, but there was a woman sitting at a reception desk.

I smiled at her and said, 'Miss Powers?' and when she looked at me doubtfully, I flourished my posy and said, 'I'm her brother.'

'First floor, turn left, Room 14,' she said.

I think she regretted it almost as she was saying it, but I was off running up the stairs. I turned left down a long corridor, and when I reached No. 14, I didn't hesitate but pushed open the door and stepped inside.

Mitch, pale as death, lay on a bed with Donna sitting by her side. Two pairs of eyes rounded as they registered me. Neither registered welcome.

I said something like, 'Oh Jesus, Mitch, what's happened to you?'

Donna jammed her finger onto a bell-push and demanded, 'What the hell are you doing here?'

And Mitch turned her head away and began crying.

That was as much meaningful conversation as we had before a nurse arrived followed by a security man and I found myself bundled down the stairs and out of the door.

I had to wait nearly an hour before Donna appeared. When I rode up alongside her shoulder she glanced at me, then said flatly, 'Listen to what I say because this is the last time we'll talk. Your mother told Mitch about your father being some kind of nut and warned her the condition was hereditary and you needed medication from time to time to stop you going the same way. Not surprisingly Mitch doesn't want any part of this, so consider yourself dumped.'

This was so devastating that the air seemed to go

dark and I've no recollection of the next several minutes. When I took notice of my surroundings again, we were almost back at the flat.

I said, 'But why is she in The Cedars? She looked really ill.'

Donna dismounted, chained her bike to the railings, went up the steps and opened the door.

'She had an abortion,' she said. 'There were complications, but she's okay now.'

She stepped inside, and slammed the door behind her.

I went back to my room and lay on my bed to think things through.

It didn't take long. Everything now became crystal clear. My mother had invested so much of her time and energy in binding me to her that she couldn't bear the thought that one day I must break free. As long as I was flitting from girl to girl, she didn't mind. But as soon as I started getting serious, she sat up and took notice.

It had never struck me before that love could be a destructive force, but now for the first time I wondered if it might have been some aspect of this same obsessive love that drove my father to plunge into Greendale Gorge. That was speculation. What I was now certain of was that she had told Gina and Kelly the same lies as she'd told to Mitch!

That early interference I could just about forgive. Only my pride had been hurt. But when it came to Mitch, not only had Mother ruined my hope of happiness, she had so terrified the poor girl that she had ended up in The Cedars, destroying our unborn child and almost losing her own life.

I felt my mind spinning out of control and I reached

for my capsules. As I took them, I recalled my
mother's reluctance in handing them over to me for
self-administration when I left for the university. Now
I understood that in her eyes the act must have
symbolised a relinquishment of power. Even then she
only gave me as many as she estimated I might need
in half a term, keeping the rest of the six-month
prescription 'safe at home' as she put it. Keeping *me*
safe at home was what she meant! At this moment I
hated her and never wanted to see her again.

Then my mobile rang.

It was Mother. I was so worked up, I didn't give
her the chance to speak but launched into a tirade of
abuse and accusation. When I finished there was
silence at the other end. What else could there be?
Justification? Defence? No, not even Mother, realising
she had been responsible for the death of her own
grandchild, could try that.

I said, 'Mother, I'm coming home to pick up my
things. Then I'm out of there forever. Don't try to stop
me. I can never forgive you. We're done.'

And I rang off.

I had calmed down by the time I got home. I was
sure she'd be waiting for me, ready to promise
anything in her efforts to make me change my mind.
But I was resolved. For once in my life I was going to
be the controller, not the controlled.

But she, as always, was ahead of me.

The broken capsules (my capsules, of course! she
wanted me to suffer) lay all around her chair; the
glass was still held lightly by her almost lifeless hand.
All my cold rationality fled. I could only think of
everything she had been to me all these years. There
was time for only a few words, of love and

forgiveness. Then the glass fell to the floor and her eyes closed forever.

Perhaps I should have called for help, but I fell into a trancelike paralysis of grief. When I emerged from it, I found myself sitting at her bureau, writing this letter.

I had to talk to someone, Mr Dalziel, and I thought of you. By the time you read this, I will have joined Mother in a better world. I know how and where I shall make the transition, high up on Greendale Pass where my poor father ended his life all those years ago.

Like father, like son.

All I ask of you, Mr Dalziel, is that you tell it like it is.

Yours sincerely
William Appleby

I floated in a featureless world of light and shade, myself a part of the chiaroscuro, till a strange rumbling sound like distant thunder drew me upwards and gave me once more a sense of individual being.

I opened my eyes. Before me I saw a tremendous figure, menacing, judgemental, and I was filled with fear.

'Lord?' I croaked.

'Eh?' said the figure.

I blinked. And blinked again.

The figure slowly reduced to a grossly fat man overflowing a small chair by the bed on which I lay.

I whispered, 'Sorry. Thought you were God.'

'Common mistake,' said the man. 'Name's Dalziel. NURSE!'

A nurse came bustling in. She said sharply, 'We do have bells.'

'Like a bike, you mean? Which bit of you's it fixed on?'

She took my pulse and my temperature, gave me a glass of water, and said, 'I'll tell Mr Kali the consultant you're awake. Try to rest. No talking.'

With a glower at the fat man, she left.

'I love a bossy woman in uniform,' he said.

He shifted his huge buttocks in the chair and once more I heard the rumbling sound.

'Better out than in,' he said. 'Now, Mr Appleby, William, okay if I call thee Bill? Or mebbe Willy? You wrote me a letter.'

'Did I? Yes, I remember. Oh God!'

I closed my eyes and a sob rocked my body.

'Don't tek on, Willy,' he said. 'You're a very lucky boy. Airbag saved you. Plus you can't have been going fast enough to clear the undergrowth and get a straight drop into the gorge.'

'It doesn't feel lucky,' I murmured.

'Not to worry, you're still young, all your life to kill yourself in,' he said consolingly. 'So let's see. You say you wrote to me 'cos you wanted a man who'd not be scared of the truth.'

'Yes.'

'Well, you've come to the right shop. So let's have a look at this truth, shall we? And to start off, I've got to tell you there's one or two things you've got a bit wrong. Best get them out of the way first off.'

He pulled my letter out of the inside pocket of a jacket which could have doubled as a marquee at a small wedding, and stabbed his finger at one of the pages.

'This stuff about your dad's accident. Suicide you guess. Trouble is, there were three witnesses. Walkers. Saw him skid on a patch of ice. Straight over the edge, no airbags to save him. So definitely an accident.'

'Does it make a difference?' I asked dully.

'Likely not. Except it does relate to what your mam said to put your girlfriends off you . . .'

'Oh God,' I interrupted. 'How could she tell those dreadful lies?'

'Likely her being a woman helped,' he said. 'And your mam. Plus, they weren't exactly lies.'

'I'm sorry?'

He patted my shoulder, sympathetically I suppose, but it felt like being clubbed with a baseball bat.

'Something you need to know about your dad, Willy. He weren't a very nice man. I mean, he had lots of charm, no problem getting in a girl's knickers. Bit like you. But underneath it . . . well, you'd likely not know he'd been married before when he met your mam?'

This was news to me and I said so.

'Aye, over in Lancashire, young woman, bit of money she'd inherited from her parents, plus the family house. They got wed, he soon went through the money, mortgaged the house, went through that too. Then she died. Accident. Fell down the stairs. Luckily for him he'd taken out a hefty chunk of term insurance on her. There was talk. There always is.'

'What's this got to do with anything?' I demanded.

'Just thought you might be interested. Any road, nothing proved, talk died, he moved away. But there was this old uncle, ex-cop, he didn't forget, he kept on digging. Found a similar case, down in Cheshire. Different name, but the newspaper pics looked like the same guy. Now he tracked your dad across here to Yorkshire. And when he discovered he'd got married again, he alerted the local CID chief. That's me in case you've forgotten.'

Suddenly I began to understand Dalziel's connection with Mother. I should have guessed there must have been something that kick-started her interest.

'And what steps did you take?' I demanded.

'Bloody careful ones! But when I found out that he'd taken out a big term insurance on your mam, well, I had to talk to her, didn't I? It were hard, mind you, what with her having a babbie. That 'ud be you. You were an ugly little bugger. At first your mam didn't want to believe me, but I think deep down she were already having doubts. The insurance policy came as a real shock. But afore we could decide what was best to do, your dad had his accident. The clincher came when the lawyers told her that he'd got through her own little bit of cash and most of what they'd got from mortgaging the house – it was your mam's house, did you know that?'

I shook my head.

'At least she didn't get pushed down the stairs. But she were left with a kid to bring up and not much money. In the circs I think she's done pretty well. A lot of what you say about the way she made ends meet is probably true, but after her experience, you can't blame her if she took advantage of a lot of greedy men, can you?'

'No, no,' I said faintly. 'I didn't blame her. I make that clear in my letter.'

'So you do. But this business of putting your girlfriends off, well, think about it. There's you, with all your dad's charm, girls at your beck and call, but somehow it was always the ones with a bit of money behind them that you get really close up and cosy with. Gina's dad owns a brewery, Kelly's family's got a chain of hotels, and with Mitch, you were really farting through silk. Landowners, huntin', shootin', fishin', all that crap. When your mam saw that, no wonder alarm bells rang. You'd been diagnosed borderline psychotic early on. Big mood swings, low moral sense, all right if you kept taking the medicine. She tried to keep it from you just how serious your condition was, but I think you knew, didn't you?'

I ignored his question and protested, 'But what she made Mitch do, there's no justifying that!'

'Well, she certainly spoke to Mitch, like her friend Donna told you. Doesn't much like you, that lass, happy to see you squirm, I'd guess. Thing is, Mitch didn't need to be warned off. She was ready to dump you anyway.'

'But our baby . . .' I said disbelievingly.

'Hers, not yours. Seems she'd been having a thing with one of her tutors. Hairy bugger, ranting Red, drops his aitches, even less her family's type than you, plus he's already got a wife and five bairns so wasn't going to be much enthused at the thought of another in either class. Mitch chatted to your mam about the pros and cons of termination. Not hard to guess which side your mam came down on after her experience.'

I was completely knocked back by this. I felt that otherworldly light and shade beginning to swim around me once more.

'Please,' I murmured. 'I need the nurse . . .'

'In a sec,' he said. 'Just one last thing to get sorted. Was it because you really thought your mam had buggered things up between you and Mitch that you killed her? Or was it finding the insurance policy that made up your mind?'

Suddenly I was completely back in the stark clear world of the hospital room.

'I don't understand . . .' I said.

'Aye, you do. Must have come as a real surprise when you found that policy for all that money with less than a year of its term to run. Your dad had taken it out for twenty years when he got married. He didn't want to attract suspicion by going for a really short term. And your daft, doting mam kept up the premiums all them years, even adding a bit to it when she could, all to keep you covered in case she should snuff it before you came of age. I can see how you must have thought it a shame to let all her sacrifice come to nowt. And you'd have been able to buy that motor-bike at last!'

'This is outrageous!' I protested. 'You must be mad. Nurse! Nurse!'

'Don't shout, she doesn't like it, remember,' he said. 'So you went home, made her a nice strong cup of tea, laced with the contents of your capsules. I bet you'd checked out the drug in the uni library and knew exactly how much would be a fatal dose. Soon she got dozy, and while she slipped away, you cleared away the cups, put a glass in her hand and sat down to write this letter. Then off to Greendale Gorge, crash gently through the fence, jump out of the car at the last minute, and scramble down the gorge to lie beside the wreck till you were found. Except you suddenly had a witness, the farmer in his tractor, so you had to take the risk of really going over the edge.'

'You're crazy!' I cried. 'You don't have a shred of evidence and if you dare repeat this in front of witnesses I'll sue you for every penny you have!'

'You'd not get much,' he said quietly. 'As for witnesses, well, I do have one. You see, your doting mam worried herself sick about you being away from home, having to do things for yourself, so she had some placebos made up which she mixed in with the real capsules, just to lessen the chance of you overdosing by accident. So there were enough sedative in her drink to knock her cold, but you'd have needed a lot more to kill her.'

'I don't believe you,' I said, dry mouthed.

But I was already following his gaze to the door.

It opened, and Mother came in.

She smiled at me sadly, forgivingly, even – God help me – lovingly.

But she didn't speak. What was there to say?

She'd warned me I'd make a fool of myself by writing to Dalziel.

I should have listened.

Mother is always right.

THE DETECTION CLUB –
A BRIEF HISTORY

Simon Brett

Probably the most pertinent comment about the Detection Club was made by the late Gavin Lyall, who described it as 'a Club whose strongest tradition seems to be the rewriting of its traditions'. This endearingly British habit, combined with a deep unwillingness over the years to keep proper archives, means that the history of the Detection Club is, at best, sketchy and at times purely conjectural. As a result, this is not a definitive essay on the subject, merely an assemblage of verifiable facts, feasible conjectures and downright apocrypha. And it relies heavily on the researches of other members, some of whom are still alive and some of whom have passed away to solve that Eternal Whodunnit in the Sky.

I am very honoured to be the current president of the Detection Club – honoured in particular because of the wonderful roll of names that I follow. On the Club's letterhead are listed G.K. Chesterton, E.C. Bentley, Dorothy L. Sayers, Lord Gorell, Agatha Christie, Julian Symons and H.R.F. Keating. I still can't see my name there at the end of the list without mouthing an involuntary 'Who?'

In writing of the Detection Club there is also a minor problem of confidentiality. Though not a secret society like the Freemasons, it is essentially a members' club, and there are some details that should not be made public. So, for example, while I might be very happy to reveal the method by which new members are voted in, I will not be revealing the names of defeated candidates, nor any of the reasons why they might have been defeated. I will maintain the Club's tradition of benign propriety. (Mind you, there is currently an unauthorised website which contains many details of the Detection Club, so the maintenance of any secrecy in the current age is hard.)

As is fitting for an association of its kind, the precise origins of the Detection Club are shrouded in mystery. You can read in many sources that it was founded in 1932 with twenty-six members, but this assertion is somewhat weakened by the fact that a letter was published in the *Times Literary Supplement* in 1930 and signed by members of the Detection Club. And the serials *Scoop* and *Behind the Screen* appeared in *The Listener* respectively in 1930 and 1931. They were written by multiple authors, including Agatha Christie, Dorothy L. Sayers, E.C. Bentley and Anthony Berkeley, under the name of the Detection Club.

So a more likely prehistory of the Club was that round about 1928 Anthony Berkeley and other detective writers started to meet for informal dinners, which then became more established into the rituals of a club. According to some sources, G.K. Chesterton was appointed the first president – though sometimes referred to as 'leader' – in 1930. Mind you, other authorities say that he didn't take over the presidential mantle – of which more hereafter – until 1932. In fact, on the headed Detection Club notepaper it says Chesterton's reign began in 1932, whereas in the Detection Club List of Members it says 1930. What is certain, however, is that, on 11 March 1932, the Constitution and Rules of the Detection Club were adopted.

The opening section reads: 'The Detection Club is

instituted for the association of writers of detective-novels and for promoting and continuing a mutual interest and fellowship between them.' And members had to fulfil 'the following condition: 'That he or she has written at least two detective-novels of admitted merit or (in exceptional cases) one such novel; it being understood that the term detective-novel does not include adventure-stories or thrillers or stories in which the detection is not the main interest, and that it is a demerit in a detective-novel if the author does not "play fair by the reader".'

In this 1932 Constitution, the Ordinary Meetings of the Club should be 'not fewer than four in the year', so things haven't changed that much. In 2005 – and for many years before that – the Detection Club met three times.

And what do we meet for? What indeed is the Detection Club for? This question is answered, in a way that still stands up today, by Dorothy L. Sayers in the 1931 introduction to *The Floating Admiral*, a multi-authored novel by members of the Club.

'What is the Detection Club? It is a private association of writers of detective fiction in Great Britain, existing chiefly for the purpose of eating dinners together at suitable intervals and of talking illimitable shop . . . If there is any serious aim behind the avowedly frivolous organisation of the Detection Club, it is to keep the detective story up to the highest standards that its nature permits, and to free it from the bad legacy of sensationalism, claptrap and jargon with which it was unhappily burdened in the past.'

So who were the members of this 'avowedly frivolous organisation' who would join each other for convivial dinners in the early 1930s? Well, they were then – as they are now – the cream of British detective writing. G.K. Chesterton, obviously; Agatha Christie, Dorothy L. Sayers, Anthony

Berkeley (later, of course, to write as Francis Iles), Freeman Wills Croft, Clemence Dane, R. Austin Freeman, Ronald Knox, A.E.W. Mason, A.A. Milne, Baroness Orczy . . . The founding members make up an impressive list, by any standards. Then E.R. Punshon joined in 1933, Margery Allingham in 1934, and the American John Dickson Carr – the only non-British author ever to have been a member – joined the Club in 1936.

The Second World War took its toll on many institutions and the Detection Club was not spared. There is no record of any dinners during that period, and certainly no new members were elected between 1937 and 1946.

In the pre-war period – the 1930s are often referred to as 'the Golden Age of crime fiction' – the Club flourished, and even had permanent club rooms in London where the members could meet up and discuss their craft or, as is still the case nowadays, anything else that came into their minds. In the 1930s, the major dinner, when new members were initiated, was usually held at the Café Royal, but other venues were used for less formal meetings.

After the war, through Dorothy L. Sayers' influence with the Church authorities, a room was rented in Kingly Street for the use of members, and it is recorded that Christianna Brand, elected to the Club in 1946, used to 'produce various delicacies in the way of food'.

But the 1940s were no longer the 'Golden Age' of whodunnit puzzles set at country-house parties, where a murder was no more than a key to set a clockwork machinery in motion. Attitudes had changed, and the very future of the crime novel was under threat. I don't think it's too extreme to compare the position of crime fiction at the time to that of representational painting after the invention of photography. Its previous role seemed to be redundant, so the form could either disappear, or change. I'm glad to say that both painting and the crime novel changed, and found even more potential in their new incarnations.

Greater reality and greater psychological understanding came into crime fiction. The genre opened out into other areas: espionage, the journalistically accurate thriller. And, inevitably, with these changes came an increasing moral ambivalence. Readers were no longer satisfied with a tale ended by Hercule Poirot in the library pointing a finger at some bounder, the loose ends of whose story would be conveniently tied into a noose by the hangman.

There was more interest in the motivation of the criminal, even sympathy for the circumstances that might lead someone to commit a murder. What had been a world of black and white was now a blurred landscape of unsettling greys.

Inevitably, the post-war change in attitude to the crime novel had its effect on the Detection Club, and that effect is well described in Julian Symons' introduction to the 1981 anthology, *Verdict of Thirteen*:

'The years of peace saw a dramatic decline in the detective story as the founders had conceived it, and this decline was mirrored in the Club's fortunes. It had always depended on the intense enthusiasm of a few members, and now as these members died, or ceased writing, or lost interest, the numbers coming to meetings fell away . . . This was true especially after the death of Sayers in 1957 . . .

'The dismal years were ended by two decisions. The first was to acknowledge that the old rules could no longer apply, and to broaden the membership to include the best writers in all forms of crime literature, including the spy story and the thriller. The other was the inspired suggestion that all dinners, except that at which new members were inaugurated, should be held in a club. This idea was an immediate success, and for several years now meetings have been held in the pleasant ambience of the Garrick Club, although the dinner for new members still takes place at the Café Royal.'

Since the time Julian wrote that, though the Garrick is still used twice a year, the venue for the autumn dinner has changed. For some years in the 1990s, it was held at the Savoy, then at the Middle Temple, the Ritz and currently in the splendid surroundings of the Park Suite at The Dorchester.

Who pays for all these wonderful dinners? The answer is that the members do. The Detection Club is a dining club, and one of the privileges of membership is the right to pay for your own dinner and that of your guests.

At times, though, the dinners have been subsidised, usually by royalty income from the Club's publications, of which some have already been mentioned. *The Scoop* and *Behind the Screen* were published in *The Listener*, then later broadcast, and the complete novel, *The Floating Admiral, by Certain Members of the Detection Club*, came out in 1931.

The book was very much a product of its time. As is right and proper, there is a map in the front, showing the church and the river and the railway line. Each chapter was written by a different Detection Club member, and at the end of the book most of them also offered their solutions to what happened and who had perpetrated the murder.

Dorothy L. Sayers wrote the introduction, and G.K. Chesterton the prologue. Then ensued chapters by, respectively, Canon Victor L. Whitechurch, G.D.H. and M.D. Cole, Henry Wade, Agatha Christie, John Rhode, Milward Kennedy, Dorothy L. Sayers again, Ronald Knox, Freeman Wills Croft, Edgar Jepson, Clemence Dane and Anthony Berkeley. And the copyright line reads, 'The Detection Club'.

Though a period piece, the book is surprisingly readable. Passing on the baton of narration does not have too disruptive an effect on the flow of the story, and some of the solutions offered are preposterously ingenious.

The Floating Admiral has also proved of great benefit to Detection Club funds over the years. It was reissued by Macmillan in 1981 and then in a splendid new edition by HarperCollins in 2011. It has also been translated into quite a few foreign languages. (The title in German, incidentally, for people who like a cheap laugh, is *Der Admirals Fahrt.*)

Apart from *The Floating Admiral*, there have been other books co-authored by members of the Detection Club. Titles such as *Ask a Policeman*, *The Anatomy of Murder* and *Double Death* spring to mind, though with some of these the Club imprimatur is not firmly established. For instance, in his preface to *Double Death*, which was first published in the *Sunday Chronicle* in 1939, John Chancellor did not make clear that it was a Detection Club book.

One that definitely was, though, came out in 1978, under the title *Verdict of Thirteen*. Again it had a starry line-up of contributors: P.D. James, Gwendoline Butler, Dick Francis, Michael Gilbert, Christianna Brand, Michael Innes, Patricia Highsmith, Celia Fremlin, H.R.F. Keating, Michael Underwood, Ngaio Marsh, Peter Dickinson and Julian Symons.

Also, in celebration of the last-named author's eightieth birthday, Harry Keating edited a collection of short stories from Detection Club members who had had a particular closeness to Julian. In tribute to a writer whose titles had included *The Man Who Killed Himself*, *The Man Whose Dreams Came True* and *The Man Who Lost His Wife*, Harry insisted that each story in the collection should have a title beginning *The Man Who* . . . I myself was honoured to be one of the contributors to that 'fiction Festschrift' and wrote a tale of literary skulduggery that was called *The Man Who Got The Dirt*. Other splendid titles from the anthology included Len Deighton's *The Man Who Was A Coyote*, Antonia Fraser's *The Man Who Wiped The Smile Off Her Face* and Reginald Hill's intriguing *The Man Who Defenestrated His Sister*.

So how does one become a member of the Detection Club? Well, the answer is: by no effort of one's own – except the effort of writing crime novels good enough to put one in the frame for consideration. But the election of new members is done by a genuinely secret ballot, and no one is informed that their name has even been put forward until they get a letter inviting them to join. By the same token, candidates who are not elected never even know that their names have been discussed. Certainly, since I have been involved in the Detection Club, I have never been aware of anyone lobbying to get themselves elected. Which I think is just as well, because lobbying is not behaviour that would endear anyone to the membership.

Nowhere is it written down precisely how many members of the Detection Club there should be at any given time, but in recent years it has always ended up round the fifty mark. As the numbers are reduced by what is euphemistically called 'natural wastage', so potential new members are nominated – with a proposer and seconder – and put up for election. The successful candidates then receive a letter from the current president, asking if they would like to become members.

The answer, incidentally, is not invariably yes. Some writers are not by nature gregarious; some do not relish the prospect of travelling to London; some feel their lives are already too full. But I am glad to say that the overwhelming majority of writers invited to join are delighted to accept the honour of Detection Club membership.

And when they have accepted, of course, they face the Initiation Ceremony. This is probably the most discussed aspect of the Detection Club, and many rumours abound as to the form it takes. Here, going back to my earlier caution, I have to be careful what I write. I can't give much away about the *current* Detection Club initiation ceremony, but I can take an historical perspective and say how it *used* to be. On this subject, I will be relying heavily on the late Gavin Lyall who, characteristically laconic, wrote some years ago 'A Brief Historical Monograph on the Detection Club Initiation Ceremony'.

It should be said first that the ceremony has always had a tongue-in-cheek element. When new members in the twenty-first century are asked to lay their hand on Eric the Skull and say what, in the context of their crime-writing, they hold sacred, the expectation is that they will offer something lighter than deep religious beliefs. The equally jokey original ritual was probably devised by G.K. Chesterton and Dorothy L. Sayers – though Ronald Knox may have had a hand in it too – and was much concerned with the rules of the genre in which they were writing.

Here is an extract from Gavin's monograph:

'No record of the original ritual exists in the Club's archives, but Maisie Ward's biography of Chesterton gives a version which apparently Chesterton himself had published in a small literary magazine.

'Although Ward's version may be complete in itself, it ends a little abruptly, and we should remember that it is not our own "prompt" copy and so may have been edited. But, that said, it is simple, light-hearted and short, lasting less than two minutes, and involves only the Ruler and the

Candidate. The latter is asked to agree to two statements. The first demands the forswearing of "Divine Revelation, Feminine Intuition, Mumbo Jumbo, Jiggery Pokery" in the detection of crime, the second requires moderation in using "Conspiracies, Death-Rays, Ghosts . . . Trap-Doors . . . Super-Criminals and Lunatics" among other things. This could well be a swipe at certain thriller-writers of the 1920s; it certainly makes clear what sort of authors were not welcome in the Club. And the idea of asking what thing the Candidate held sacred and to swear by that is there from the start – although the skull seems to be a later addition.

'The 1930s may have been the Club's golden age, but for our archives it is the Dark Ages – though outside sources hint at lost gold. In her memoirs, Dame Ngaio Marsh (who, living mainly in New Zealand, did not become a member till 1974) recalls being a guest at the pre-war initiation of E.C. Bentley involving Wardens of the Naked Blade, the Hollow Skull and the Lethal Phial, with Dorothy L. Sayers as president brandishing and firing off a pistol. But this may be inaccurate because Sayers did not become president until 1949 and Bentley was a founder member of the Club. However, in 1936 Bentley was inaugurated as president and so Dame Ngaio may have been remembering this ceremony, of which we have no record. And Sayers could have played the "Warden of the Firearm", for which post there is later evidence.'

A bit of detective work by Gavin Lyall and Peter Lovesey unearthed a printed version of the ceremony as it was probably used in 1937, which – quoting Gavin's monograph once again – '. . . lengthens the oath and ends on a threat for breaking it: "may total strangers sue you for libel, your pages swarm with misprints and your sales continually diminish." This text adds the now-familiar opening: "What mean these lights . . . this reminder of our Mortality?" and goes on to a sponsor mentioning the candidate's books. It also adds "Eric the Skull", the first extant mention of the name, along with a skull-bearer and several torchbearers. If our interpretation of Dame Ngaio's memory is correct, these could have been invented for the 1936 Presidential Inauguration and later carried across to the Initiation Ceremony. But there is no reference to any Wardens.

'However, in 1958 the Wardens, including those of the Firearm, Rope and the Blunt Instrument, were back in force for the inauguration of Lord Gorell as president (actually co-president with the self-effacing Agatha Christie), and to other unspecified posts. The colourful ceremony was credited to Richard Hull (elected 1946) and is full of high drama (or low comedy) delivered in mock Shakespearean lines by a dozen voices, with a "lugubrious" piano introduction.'

Here is an extract from that ceremony:

ORATOR: Who are you and why do you wander aimless with instruments of death in your hands, murder in your hearts and sorrow in your faces?

ROPE: We are members of the Detection Club. All sworn initiates.

BOWL: We bear the emblems of our trade. We do but murder in jest, poison in jest.

RING: And we are sad because we have no head.

ORATOR: No head? Are there not those who will rule you? I call upon the Warden of the Rope.

(*The Wardens enter, as called.*)

ROPE: I cannot serve. My rope is slack and my noose unknotted.

ORATOR: I call upon the Warden of the Bowl.

BOWL: I cannot serve. My bowl is empty.

ORATOR: I call upon the Warden of the Firearms.

FIREARMS: I cannot serve. My fire is quenched.
ORATOR: I call upon the Warden of the Sharp Instrument.
SHARP INSTRUMENT: I cannot serve. My edge is blunted.
ORATOR: I call upon the Warden of the Blunt Instrument.
BLUNT INSTRUMENT: I cannot serve. My hand has lost its power.

And so on, and so on . . .

I should point out that the Inauguration Ceremony when I took over the presidency from H.R.F. Keating was considerably simpler than that.

The Initiation of New Members also went through considerable metamorphoses, though lack of documentation makes it difficult to be precise about these. A version used in 1966 seems to have purged out much of the original humour, and contained ten rules for the proper conduct of crime writers, including this one: 'They must not allow two statements to contradict one another unless that contradiction proves to be an essential part of the plot.'

In the late 1960s the old Detection Club rules changed, as the qualification for membership was broadened to include writers who created 'detectives, secret service agents or other chief characters'. The whodunnit was no longer the only form that Detection Club members were allowed to write. And the Initiation Ceremony was adjusted accordingly. Back to Gavin Lyall's monograph:

'By this time the Club's standards had been, as one might put it, changed. Writers of books not solely concerned with detection were being admitted, and although there are references in the Club minutes to inauguration changes made in 1969, these new writers do not seem to have been fully acknowledged until a total revision in 1977. Following the by-now classic opening, the president (then Julian Symons) gave a description of the traditional murder mystery, then handed over to readers who recited brief rules for the spy story, the police procedural, the adventure, and an appeal in favour of the Queen's English. There followed encomia on the candidates' work and the oath was taken.'

There were further changes to the ceremony in the early 1980s and the new version was used when, in 1985, H.R.F. Keating took over the presidency from Julian Symons. Characteristically impish, Harry had written the rubric in verse.

Since then, the wording of the Initiation Ceremony has changed yet again – back to Gavin Lyall's line about 'a Club whose strongest tradition seems to be the rewriting of its traditions' – but I will draw a veil over its current form. Some secrets, as I said, should not be shared.

One element of apparent continuity in the Detection Club is the Presidential Robe, a rather splendid quasi-academic gown in red satin, as worn by the president at the Initiation of New Members. Cut on generous lines, one would naturally assume that it was so tailored to accommodate the substantial frame of G.K. Chesterton, the founding president or leader. And one would assume that it would have coped well with the bulk of Dorothy L. Sayers too.

Alas, one's assumptions would be wrong. The original robe was lost after a dinner at the Savoy in the 1960s, and rumour has it that the hotel paid to have a facsimile made. So, the gown I wear at the autumn dinners is a fake. Like everything else about the Detection Club, the mythology is once again blurred and unreliable . . . which I must say I find one of the most enduring – and endearing – qualities of the organisation.

To conclude then: the Detection Club has always been a lively association of crime novelists, which does not take itself too seriously, and whose sole purpose is to have convivial dinners. It is emphatically not a trades union and has no aim to raise the profile of crime-writing or of individual crime writers. The Club's ceremonies and usages may have changed over eighty-five years, but I like to think that the basic spirit in which Anthony Berkeley and others founded it has remained intact.

ALSO AVAILABLE

THE FLOATING ADMIRAL

*By Members of The Detection Club
including Agatha Christie & Dorothy L. Sayers
Preface by G.K. Chesterton*

Inspector Rudge does not encounter many cases of murder in the sleepy seaside town of Whynmouth. But when an old sailor lands a rowing boat containing a fresh corpse, the Inspector's investigation immediately comes up against several obstacles. The vicar, who owns the boat, is clearly withholding information, and the victim's niece has disappeared—even the identity of the victim is called into doubt. Inspector Rudge begins to wonder if there isn't more to this case than meets the eye . . .

In this rare collaboration by Agatha Christie, Dorothy L. Sayers and ten other crime writers from the newly-formed Detection Club, each author wrote one chapter, leaving G.K. Chesterton to supply a prologue and Anthony Berkeley to tie up all the loose ends. In addition, each of the authors provided their own solution in a sealed envelope, published at the end of the novel, with Agatha Christie's ingenious conclusion acknowledged to be "enough to make the book worth buying on its own."

This new edition is introduced by the Detection Club's current President, the author Simon Brett, who investigates the background to this extraordinary collaboration of the crime-writing fraternity.

ALSO AVAILABLE

ASK A POLICEMAN

*By Members of The Detection Club
including Dorothy L. Sayers & Gladys Mitchell
Preface by Agatha Christie*

Lord Comstock is a barbarous newspaper tycoon with enemies in high places. His murder poses a dilemma for the Home Secretary: with suspicion falling on the Chief Whip, an Archbishop, and the Assistant Commissioner for Scotland Yard, the impartiality of any police investigation is threatened. Abandoning protocol, he invites four famous detectives to solve the case: Mrs Adela Bradley, Sir John Saumarez, Lord Peter Wimsey, and Mr Roger Sheringham. All are on their own – and none of them can ask a policeman . . .

This unique whodunit involved four of the 1930s' best crime writers swapping their usual detectives and indulging in sly parodies of each other. It is introduced by Martin Edwards, archivist of the Detection Club, and includes an exclusive preface by Agatha Christie, 'Detective Writers in England', in which she discusses Sherlock Holmes, Hercule Poirot, and her Detection Club colleagues.

ALSO AVAILABLE

THE ANATOMY OF MURDER

*By Members of The Detection Club
including Francis Iles, Helen Simpson
& Dorothy L. Sayers*

As aficionados of even the most gruesome crime fiction will testify, nothing beats the horror of the real thing. True crime stories have inspired murder mystery writers from the very earliest days of detective fiction, but what happens when you ask the best authors to recreate the most infamous true crimes as if they were fiction?

From the dark streets of Pimlico and Paris to the exotic reaches of Sydney and Adelaide, some of the world's most notorious murders are here retold by seven of the most accomplished crime writers of their generation:

Helen Simpson	•	*The Death of Henry Kinder*
John Rhode	•	*The Crimes of Constance Kent*
Margaret Cole	•	*The Case of Adelaide Bartlett*
E.R. Punshon	•	*An Impression of the Landru Case*
Dorothy L. Sayers	•	*The Murder of Julia Wallace*
Francis Iles	•	*The Rattenbury Case*
Freeman Wills Crofts	•	*A New Zealand Tragedy*

This compelling fourth collection from the archives of the illustrious Detection Club, finally back in print after more than 75 years, includes a new introduction by Martin Edwards

ALSO AVAILABLE

SIX AGAINST THE YARD

*By Members of The Detection Club
including Margery Allingham & Dorothy L. Sayers
with Superintendent Cornish of the CID*

Is the 'perfect murder' possible? Can that crime be committed with such consummate care, with such exacting skill, that it is unsolvable—even to the most astute investigator?

In this unique collection, legendary crime writers Margery Allingham, Anthony Berkeley, Freeman Wills Crofts, Ronald Knox, Dorothy L. Sayers and Russell Thorndike each attempt to create the unsolvable murder mystery, which real-life Superintendent Cornish of Scotland Yard then attempts to unravel.

This clever literary battle of wits from the archives of the Detection Club follows *The Floating Admiral* and *Ask a Policeman* back into print after more than 75 years, and shows some of the experts from the Golden Age of detective fiction at their most ingenious.

For true crime aficionados, this new edition includes an essay by Agatha Christie, one of the inaugural members of the Detection Club. Unseen since 1929, her article discusses the infamous Croydon Poisonings, a real-life perfect murder, the solution to which remains a mystery to this day . . .